SEEING
THINGS

NANCY YOUNG

World Castle Publishing, LLC
Pensacola, Florida
Copyright © Nancy Young 2014
Print ISBN: 9781629891446
eBook ISBN: 9781629891453
First Edition World Castle Publishing, LLC, September 15, 2014
http://www.worldcastlepublishing.com

Licensing Notes

Cover: Karen Fuller
Editor: Katrina Haritos

Acknowledgments

I owe a debt to the many authors whose work I include in homage and parody: Edgar Allan Poe's "The Fall of the House of Usher," Daphne du Maurier's *Rebecca*, Charlotte Brontë's *Jane Eyre*, Jane Austen's *Northanger Abbey*, Charlotte Perkins Gilman's "The Yellow Wallpaper," and, of course, the quote from and nods to Shirley Jackson's *The Haunting of Hill House* (published by Penguin Classics, cover design by Roseanne J. Serra, cover illustration by Harry Bliss).

While the Internet captions at chapter heads are fiction, they reflect actual kinds of postings and historical facts gleaned from web sites, newspaper accounts, and old documents. Sometimes reality is stranger than fiction. In addition, although the specific locations and people in this novel are fictitious, the backdrop of the Main Line and its time-honored traditions are very real.

Without the prodding, the looming deadlines, and the invaluable suggestions from my writing group (Laura Towne, Jack Lloyd, and Jan B. Parker), this novel would never have been completed. And without the patience and support of my family, I'd never have had the fortitude to start. Therefore, I owe a deep debt to Dan for his love and support, to Dylan for my web site, to Sarah for her advice, to Katie for her enthusiasm, to Danny for listening to the book on road trips, and to Tim, who always knows what a snarky teen would say in any situation, natural or supernatural.

CHAPTER ONE

Internet Results: *Characteristics of a Haunted House*
Shuttered, decaying, and isolated, the typical haunted mansion seeps atmosphere. Hollywood prefers the Gothic or Tudor, though any classic creepy-looking manse will do — especially if a menacing iron fence surrounds it and it beckons under a threatening sky.

Smiling down at the text, I had to admit he got it mostly right. This whole job interview felt like the setup for a cheap Gothic romance.

Ahead of me, Grey Crag dominated the crest of the Devon hillside, an uneasy mix of Victorian, Tudor, and Romanesque, gabled and mullioned to its red tile rooftops. But the granite walls looked sturdy enough, the windows were neither vacant nor eyelike, the sky blared blue with no hint of storm, and I felt nothing more ominous than a faint pain from sitting too long. "Tally ho," I muttered, unbuckling the seat belt.

Gothic heroines probably spring lithe and willowy from their bucket seats, but I squeezed out from behind the steering wheel, tugging my jacket to hide that I was more maple than willow.

I really needed this job.

The stone steps led me through a double archway, beyond which loomed the portal—no mere door for Grey Crag. What name would suit the rental D.J. and I shared in Malvern? Bungle-low, maybe? From a nearby pillar, an honest-to-God gargoyle glared over my shoulder as I pressed the brass doorbell, triggering Westminster chimes to echo through passageways beyond. Taking advantage of the wait, I checked my reflection in the sidelight windows framing the door. The limp hair looked a little reddish in the afternoon sunlight instead of its usual boring brown. I smoothed flyaway strands, straightened my tortoiseshell glasses, buttoned the navy blazer, sucked in my stomach, and adjusted the matching skirt, which had a tendency to ride up over my expanding hips. There. I looked cool, calm, and professional. I could pull this off.

Considering the setting, I expected a cadaverous Mrs. Danvers clone to answer the bell.

Instead, a chubby tabby swished across the flagstones to squeak expectantly. "Pushy beast, aren't you?" While bent to stroke the welcoming committee, bottom to the door, I heard a scuffle and the creak of hinges.

"Mrs. Livingston, I presume."

So much for first impressions. I shored up my drooping dignity, upped the amps of my wide smile, and held out my hand. "Mrs. Parrish?"

The woman answering the door looked frail, but her grip could take down an Amazon. "So happy to meet you. And I see you've already met Penrod." She glanced down at the twitching tail and back at me. "Have any trouble finding us?"

"Hard to miss the place." I wasn't exaggerating. Along this stretch of lane, the landscape bore only the mansion and a few well-trimmed trees. "And I grew up not too far from here, in a subdivision up Waterloo Road."

"Well, welcome back to Pennsylvania, then. Please, come in." The cat stalked through the arched doors to a wide hallway. "I don't think I included you," the owner chided. Penrod didn't seem to take offense.

I suppose the echoing space was more a foyer or even a narthex, since its dimensions shouted cathedral. D.J.'s dire predictions proved true again. The ceiling above us rose twenty feet, timbered in dark wood. The same wood gleamed under rectangles of Oriental carpeting in cabernet red.

I'd been prepared for the grandeur, but not the light that bounced off the carved paneling, parquet floor, and marble fireplace. It warmed the stained glass in the first bend of the massive staircase and made a halo of the white curls crowning Mrs. Parrish's head.

"Rather much at first sight, isn't it?" she laughed. "Even I'm overwhelmed sometimes, and I've lived here most of my life."

I couldn't imagine a miniature Mrs. Parrish growing up in such a place. "You must love it here." I consciously resisted the urge to run a hand over the smooth wood. "It's so majestic and peaceful."

"That's what my father always said. He called it his haven, his retreat from the city." She stared at the mantelpiece without seeing. "He never wanted to leave." She nodded her head, a faraway look in her eyes. "My husband felt the same way."

"I can certainly understand that." I felt a little uneasy about the mantelpiece urn that seemed to capture her attention. "I'm eager to hear more about the position."

"Let's go into the library, then. It's nice and cheerful this time of morning." Despite her age, the woman made good time across the checkerboard of carpets through an archway

9

beyond the staircase. "I have some coffee and sweet rolls all ready."

The spread on the refectory table alone was enough to convince me I wanted this gig. Ahead, the cat leaped up to inspect the offerings. Shooing him away, his owner gestured to a nearby settee flanking a second fireplace. "Please make yourself comfortable, Mrs. Livingston. It's softer than it looks."

"You know, much of your home strikes me just that way. Surprisingly inviting." I settled in and accepted a cup. I could get used to this.

"So you feel it, then," her hostess nodded. "Some do right away."

"I've never really considered myself the sensitive type." I sipped cautiously and tugged my skirt.

Mrs. Parrish smiled. "That may well work in your favor. The last person in the position turned out to be a bit too sensitive."

I laughed. "No one's ever accused me of that." Except my cheating, porno-obsessed ex-husband. I decided to leave that part out.

"There are all kinds of sensitivity, Mrs. Livingston." Her smile had deepened, revealing an impressive set of dentures. "So let's get down to business. I see that you can drive."

I smiled back. "I can. I also possess excellent verbal and written skills and considerably more than a high school GED," I added. "I enjoy reading and researching. I can bend, stoop, push, reach, sit, and walk with no problem, and I can heft a weight greater than Penrod here if required."

Mrs. Parrish chuckled, a creaky sound that matched the door hinges. "You must have memorized the ad."

"Ma'am, this companion job and I are a perfect fit in every way."

"Perhaps you wouldn't mind a little audition?"

"Excuse me?"

"I don't see as well as I'd like, but I do enjoy books." She nodded to the volumes that lined the library shelves. "As you can tell, a love of literature runs in my family. Do you have a favorite author, Mrs. Livingston?"

"I'm sure I couldn't pick just one," I answered, hoisting myself from the settee to scan the titles, mostly leather-bound classic sets of Shakespeare, Dickens, Hardy, and Doyle. "I like a variety—Austen, the Brontës, of course. Tim O'Brien, Kurt Vonnegut, Toni Morrison, Angela Carter, early Stephen King…" Pausing, I selected a copy of the Shirley Jackson novel I'd taught a few years before. "I love this book." After wiping my glasses, I read the opening lines aloud, finishing with "*silence lay steadily against the wood and stone of Hill House, and whatever walked there, walked alone.*"

Mrs. Parrish's smile hadn't dimmed. "Yes, I think you'll fit right in," she said. With exactly what, she didn't say.

CHAPTER TWO

Squeezed again into the front seat, I wasted no time in texting the one person most likely to care. "I got it. Start packing." I was already calculating how many additional boxes I'd need. I'd probably lose the deposit on the rental house, but scoring free room and board, along with a living wage, more than made up for the loss. Most importantly, we'd be settled into one of the best school districts in the state before Labor Day.

D.J., of course, failed to appreciate these benefits, a fact he made clear after I pulled into the cracked driveway of the rental. He was waiting on the stoop like an angry chaperone whose charge left the prom to make out in the parking lot.

"God, Mom, we just moved in." His voice cracked from an infusion of fury and puberty. "Do you ever stop and think about how I feel?"

His tone and phrasing perfectly matched his father's when I'd walked out on him months earlier. Oddly enough, I felt no more compelled to placate the boy than I had the man, insensitive bitch that I am. "Here, take these inside," I answered, thrusting a bag in his arms. "And don't squish them."

He peered into the bag. "What's in here?"

"A sampling of the kind of eating you can look forward to in the new place," I tossed back. "Not that I was thinking about you or anything." I softened somewhat. "Try the sticky bun. It's a local classic."

"Man, there are three kinds of danishes in here. And an éclair." The last phrase was muffled as he stuffed the pastry into his mouth.

I plopped down next to him on the stoop, brushing his hair off his face so I could find his eyes. "There's more where that came from. Lots more."

"This doesn't make it right, you know." He bit into the cherry danish.

"Helps, though, doesn't it?" I firmly tamped the guilt down and forged on. "And we'll pretty much have a whole wing to call our own. Wait till you see this place."

"Already did." D.J. managed to smirk with a full mouth. "Google street view."

"So?"

"Looks like that place in *Rocky Horror*."

"You're too young to watch *Rocky Horror*. And it's nothing like that place. That was a creepy castle."

He looked up, his blue gaze pinning me. "And your point is?"

"D.J., this is the best I can do. We'll have a great place to live, great food, a steady income…"

"We had that stuff before."

He was right. He used to live in a safe home with a fully stocked refrigerator and a father in residence. He'd lost all of that because of me. Never mind that his father had turned into a roaming hound with increasingly disturbing preferences that I could no longer overlook. I squelched the input signal replaying the day I found a size five purple thong underneath our bed. Then I tried gating a flood of other memories — David's scathing list of my sexual inadequacies, my pitiful efforts to please, kneeling at his feet, promising to do anything and discovering I had nothing he wanted anymore.

Not that my professional life was any better. The junior college where I had worked was in lockdown at least once a month, and I had been downing antidepressants like they were breath mints.

A failing marriage, a classroom full of potential psychopaths, and a judgmental adolescent would've been enough to drive anyone to seek peace through pharmacology, right? Unfortunately, even in a medicinal fog, my problems persisted. I've always latched on for security, and the ground was breaking up beneath me.

If you keep doing the same thing, nothing changes. I don't know which talk show I heard that on, but it stuck with me because it had that zing of Truth that jolts you like a blue light in the rearview mirror. Sometimes you just can't look away from the car wreck. Since change seemed my only sane option, I escaped my crumbling landscape and hurled towards a different life full throttle. Unfortunately for D.J., he'd been hijacked along on the voyage.

"It'll be different, but that doesn't mean it won't be good, kiddo." I cringed at the pleading note in my voice.

"Good for you, maybe." He stood up, grabbed the bag, and slammed through the screen door.

Obviously I had a talent for making men miserable whether they were fourteen or forty. After grabbing my purse and locking the car, I followed D.J. inside. He had thrown himself onto the ugly brown sofa, ignoring my entrance in favor of a video game. I imagined each shot at the screen was meant for me.

Conceding this round, I kicked off the sensible navy pumps, shrugged out of the tight blazer, and crossed the room to the cramped kitchen to brew a pot of tea. Brewing tea represents stability and order. God knows I needed both. I chose a zingy lemon blend for an afternoon boost. If I'd been the mature heroine in one of those journey-to-self-discovery books, I'd be off learning Italian or discovering love in a seaside cottage or joining a cadre of kooky females on a road trip to a dude ranch. Instead, I pulled my notebook out of my purse and began a list.

Lists are another sign of stability and order. I rely on lists. That lengthy pro-con list led me away to this seedy suburb. A list of my meager talents led me to the companion position with Mrs. Parrish. And a good list would point me to true north and keep me from beating my head against the counter right now. I jotted down tasks: contacting the landlord, forwarding mail, renting another trailer, getting D.J. registered for school, and having him call David with our new address. After briefly considering that I'd been gone all morning and remembering his father's habits, I added two more to the list: *check search history* and *get boxes from the liquor store*.

I figured when all this was done and I had secured a paycheck, I'd deserve a celebratory drink too. Other than kitchen essentials, toiletries, electronic devices, and clothing, we hadn't really unpacked. The rental house always seemed stubbornly temporary, as if it resented any attempt to personalize it. Likewise, D.J. hadn't made any friends in the neighborhood, preferring to stay connected online with friends back home.

Home. I had to stop thinking of that tidy brick colonial in North Carolina as home. No one was feeding the roses or filling the hummingbird feeder. The comforters had not been sent to the cleaners. And I really didn't want to know what was happening on my high thread count sheets. Did I?

No. Time to cut bait and sail on. Odd how a cliché can creep in when you least expect it. It was like we'd left the Badlands behind and booked a cruise. We'd brave choppy seas in the week ahead, but we were out of the doldrums. Grinning, I doodled a sailboat in the margin of my list.

"So, Mom." D.J. slouched over to the counter. He was already a head taller than me and built lean. He had his dad's sunlight coloring instead of my basic beige. At this moment, I couldn't find any of me in him. I sketched a shark fin in the water around the boat.

"Son?" I was determined to win this round.

"When exactly are you expecting us to move to the Halls of Horror?"

I was tempted to mention that if he rolled his eyes too much, they might get stuck, but I showed some restraint. "We should be able to get this all packed up by Friday," I said instead. "Or sooner, depending on how much you help."

When he was two, those eyes had been windows to his soul, but now they took another turn around his sockets. "You're always after me to do stuff."

"Terrible, isn't it? You are without a doubt the most ill-treated, disadvantaged, unappreciated minion in Malvern." I suddenly remembered I'd left out the most important feature of our new home. I worked to keep my tone casual, though I knew this might be the deciding factor in the move, from D.J.'s perspective. "By the way, this place has something you can't have here."

"My very own vampire?"

"A cat."

D.J. smiled. It passed for a smile, anyway. He'd always wanted a pet, but his father had allergies to more than just monogamy. The cat had tipped the balance in Grey Crag's favor. "The end of the week. You do know what day that is, don't you, Mom?"

"The day after Thursday?"

"It's Friday the Thirteenth."

Lucky us.

CHAPTER THREE

Internet Results: *Shadow Figures*
Shadow people are among the most often reported paranormal phenomena. While some claim they are hallucinations or tricks of the light, others believe these flickering figures are truly malevolent.

The shadow in the corner didn't really look like a human figure. It was just my imagination, probably unleashed by exhaustion. I was beyond tired in body and mind, not that I'd admit to it publicly. But alone in this out-of-the-way parlor, I had let my body slump in the armchair and my mind wander.

No, it didn't really look like a figure. It must be a trick of the light as it filtered at odd angles through the jutting Victorian furnishings. The head-like knob at the top might come from the plaster medallion hanging from the high ceiling, and the arm probably resulted from the way the late afternoon sun pushed through the heavy green drapes behind me. That's all. No dark figure lurked in the shadows. There was no body. It was just an optical illusion, a projection from my overactive imagination. I was obviously overtired. And that celebratory shot I'd downed upstairs must be having an effect.

It had taken two trips for D.J. and me to load and move our belongings down Paoli Pike, past aging cookie-cutter subdivisions, around a series of bends along a narrow lane, and up the drive to Grey Crag. Item by item, I had ticked off my checklist, turning in keys and signing papers until I'd cleared all the hurdles. We'd even managed to keep pretty much on schedule in order to get the U-Haul back to the lot before it closed.

Of course, we'd lost some time on the first run while D.J. gawked at the estate, abandoning his hardened teen shell for once. Over the week, his attitude towards the move had gone through a puzzling transformation, a change I didn't want to examine too closely. His enthusiasm and my suspicions grew simultaneously. When we stood in the drive looking up at the mansion, he had that same look on his face that Carter must have had when he first looked in King Tut's tomb. And our new home was indeed full of marvelous things. While under the Grey Crag spell, D.J. even managed, unprompted, a handshake and pleasant greeting for Mrs. Parrish. This move definitely had advantages.

The kid had already made a friend of sorts. As he grudgingly hauled boxes, Penrod darted after him. So maybe this cheerful disposition was temporary, but the new start had been promising, all in all. Yes, it had been a good day, and I lazed, guilt-free, as the sun set.

David and I used to sit like this on the porch swing on summer evenings after dinner, thigh to thigh, sharing the day's dramas — his from the agency, mine from the classroom. For just a moment, I allowed myself to wonder what was happening two states away inside that brick house. Would David be cracking open a beer on the patio? Would some anorexic aviation blonde be sipping cheap rosé from my wedding crystal?

The hour between day and night always unsettled me. I knew that there was nothing in the dark that wasn't there in the light, but somehow, I didn't find that knowledge comforting. In the dark, things can sneak up on you, or you can stumble on them unexpectedly. If you confront them, they can bite. It takes a concentrated exercise of the will to refuse to acknowledge what you suspect may be there.

As a girl, at this time of day, I'd always made sure I was upstairs, beyond the lengthening shadows, above the gathering storm in the living room. When the sun hit the horizon, my mother hit the bottle of scotch, drinking herself blind. I generally hit my room, even if the neighborhood kickball game outside continued until it was dark. But I was safe here in this mansion, I reminded myself. For all intents and purposes, I was home. Well, for now.

* * *

Earlier in the afternoon, when all the boxes had been unloaded, Mrs. Parrish and Penrod had escorted D.J. on a tour of the first floor. I'd never seen him have such an interest in architecture and history. Before long, he had my employer in the library reciting her genealogy and showing him pictures of the house and its inhabitants over the years. I hoped he was keeping a lid on his mouth. We both needed the promised paycheck.

Feeling a chill, I stomped on the idea of someone walking over my grave and sank more firmly into the red leather, tugging at my rumpled shorts and tuning out my aching muscles and the faint rustles about the room. While I focused on my lethargy, I tried to identify the sounds: old ashes sifting in the fireplace or the brush of dry branches against the windows, perhaps. A distant skittering across the dining room floor through the archway to my right sharpened my attention and made me look.

21

Craning my sore neck to detect the source of the noise, I spied Penrod, striped tail erect, batting something solid across the polished floor. The object slid left and right between his paws, then skated across the room and into the grand hallway beyond. It hit the wall with a solid thunk.

Cats aren't the only creatures that can't curb their curiosity. I admire cats. They strike me as fundamentally undomesticated and opportunistic. Eons past, I imagine they skulked around the perimeters of camp fires, lingering until they spied an opportunity to insinuate themselves, ensuring a steady supply of food and soft surfaces. My own curiosity got the better of me as I stood up to see what Penrod had captured.

Muscles complaining, I traced the cat's solo soccer match as it advanced to the foot of the staircase. Above me, the jeweled stained glass spilled deep red pools on the hardwood below thanks to the sun. Penrod crouched in the middle of one bloody spot, staring past me at the landing. Unnerved, I bent to examine the object he'd abandoned.

Penrod's plaything was dark and curved. Four pointed tines stabbed my palm as I cupped it. In the dim light from a wall sconce, I identified it as an ornamental comb, the kind my mother had worn to secure her French twist in those elegant years of up-dos. This comb weighed heavier in my hand than the plastic variety, however. It could be celluloid or even tortoiseshell, given the carved rosettes along its peak. It was certainly antique.

"Took your toy, didn't I?" Penrod shifted his unwavering green gaze to me.

"Is that you, Mrs. Livingston?" Mrs. Parrish called from the library at the other end of the hall. I wondered briefly who else she thought it might be before answering.

"Yes, Mrs. Parrish," I called back. "Just looking at what the cat dragged in." My voice sounded hollow as it echoed off the paneling.

Mrs. Parrish made her way down the hall to my side and looked askance at Penrod. "Catch something interesting this time?" she asked. I held out the odd comb while the cat stalked over to the hallway fireplace and coiled gracefully to wash his back.

"Oh, my. I wonder where that came from," Mrs. Parrish warbled, stroking a bent forefinger over the intricate carving.

D.J. crowded in. "What is it, Mom? Let me see." His head blocked the light. I nudged him to one side.

"It's an old-fashioned hair comb."

"A comb? It's too bent and spiky to be a comb." He crowded in again.

"It's the fancy kind women used to use a long time ago to pin their hair. Do you recognize it, Mrs. Parrish?"

The older woman remained still as she turned the comb over, a tremor in her hand. "Why, I believe this must have belonged to my Aunt Beatrice. She had such lovely long hair in her younger days—never let a scissor near it, even when bobs were all the rage." She smiled slightly, remembering. "She used to let me brush it and braid it when I was little."

"Did she live here too?" D.J. was never shy about asking anything.

"Her whole life, with the exception of a few years when she married and moved to Bryn Mawr. Her poor husband didn't last long. Influenza, you know." She lapsed into the memory.

I leaned towards D.J., who looked puzzled. "That's the flu," I whispered.

"He died of the flu?" What D.J. lacked in tact he made up for in volume. "People can die from that?"

Mrs. Parrish's gaze reminded me of Penrod's, focused and unwavering. However, her gaze was directed at something behind us, something I couldn't see. "Yes, people can die. They can die from that—and a great many other things, I'm afraid."

D.J. couldn't suppress his ghoulish streak. "Is Beatrice dead too? Where'd she die? Here?"

"D.J., hush, you little cretin," I hissed. "I'm so sorry, Mrs. Parrish. He needs a refresher course in sensitivity."

Mrs. Parrish's smile resurfaced, though her faded blue eyes remained sad as they looked at D.J. "I believe I explained to your mother that being overly sensitive is no virtue here, young man." She handed the comb back to me. "Yes, my Aunt Beatrice came back to Grey Crag during the war, when I was around eight. She was all I had for a long time after my parents—. Well, she was still here when I married my dear Matthew, but by then she'd turned a little queer." She paused, eyes fixed. "Poor Beatrice breathed her last just down the hall from where you and your mother moved in this afternoon, as a matter of fact."

D.J.'s insensitive face lit up. "Cool! Can I go see where?"

"D.J.!" How could I have given birth to this child? And why didn't I drown him in infancy?

"Well, I—I suppose, if you like. It's the door at the end of the hall directly above the library—the one with the bay window." She looked overhead. "They said Aunt Beatrice was never the same after Uncle Willy passed. She suffered so from grief. From loneliness. It all took its toll. As the years went by, she kept more and more to her room, kind of, oh, perhaps 'nesting' is the term for it."

D.J. had already bolted up the stairs and reached the wide landing. "Coming, Mom?"

"I guess." Apparently my kid needed a keeper as well as a muzzle. I looked at my employer with an apologetic shrug and set the comb on the mantel next to the urn. Trailing Penrod, I climbed past the landing, turning again and again until I reached the next floor, where the hallway stretched for leagues in either direction. I had to stop to catch my breath.

* * *

D.J. was already halfway down our section of the corridor, his thin form barely visible since no one had thought to leave the hall lights burning in anticipation of the night. Unnerved, I hurried to catch up with him as he reached the open doorway at the end.

Penrod had stopped in front of D.J.'s room and was carefully licking his paws, as if washing himself clean of the whole adventure. I've always thought that cats have more sense than humans. Admittedly, I was feeling zero at the bone when I saw my only child walk through that dark entrance. Even the hall felt clammy and chill. I rubbed the goose bumps on my arm, and then, with a calming breath and stiffened spine, I followed him.

Once inside the chamber, I realized the darkness was an illusion. A semicircle of windows at the far end of the bedroom extended from floor to ceiling, and the last rays of day burned through, negating the need to locate the light switch. D.J. had moved to the opposite wall.

"Do you think she died right in that bed?" I could tell my boy's appetite for horror remained unsated.

"If she did, I'm sure they've changed the sheets since then, so don't get your hopes up." The massive mahogany headboard loomed against the papered wall to my right, rising like a tombstone nearly to the ceiling. Bed curtains hung like winding cloths from the canopy. Even my similes had become tainted by the place, I thought.

"Jeez, that bed's, like, half the size of my old room," D.J. marveled. "Mom, check it out."

The sunlight was fading fast as I stepped closer. And I'd put two shots in my celebratory cocktail. Also, as I mentioned, it had been a very long day. Those are the only explanations I'm giving for what I saw when I approached that vast white bed.

Chapter Four

At first, I thought it was a dark stain marring the rumpled counterpane. A step closer, and I watched the blotch resolve itself into something more closely resembling a bull's eye or a target, with a dark outer ring and a roundish center. The last step revealed the circle was actually fashioned from a tangled nest of what looked like long black hair. Within that nest huddled something unhealthy, shriveled, and, God help me, bald.

"Mom? Mom? You okay?" Long-ingrained habit made me turn from the thing in the bed towards my son. When I glanced back, the figure I thought I'd glimpsed had dissolved into sheets and shadows once more.

I really had to lay off the hard stuff.

"Of course I'm okay," I snapped, more sharply than I intended. "But I think we've indulged your lust for the macabre long enough, kid," I added as I hustled him forward and pulled the heavy door shut behind us. "We need to get back downstairs to Mrs. Parrish." Knowing food was a great motivator, I noted, "You must be getting hungry." Down the hall, Penrod hadn't vacated his spot, though his tail now twitched erratically.

Oblivious as only an adolescent boy can be, D.J. kept up a steady stream of chatter while we retraced our steps to find Mrs. Parrish still lingering by the stairs. I felt a twinge when I spied her from above, alone and vulnerable. Here I was supposed to be a paid companion, and already I'd abandoned my charge in favor of our shameful, mean-spirited inspection. Although my official duties didn't start until Saturday, I hoped she wouldn't hold this lapse against me.

"Did you find it?" she asked, voice quavering.

"The room at the very end of the hall, right?" D.J. answered.

"It's a charming room, bright and airy," I added, desperately trying to erase the image of that occupied bed. "And the sunset through the windows is just glorious."

Mrs. Parrish brightened considerably. "Yes, that's the west end of the house. The view is splendid from that wing. It's also worth seeing from the front balcony."

"Another night we'll have to go look. But it must be getting on to dinner time by now, isn't it?"

D.J. looked up from his cell phone. "It's 7:23. And Mom, there's a call from Dad." He held the phone out. Mrs. Parrish saw me wince.

"D.J., why don't I show you a shortcut to the kitchen? Your mother can join us in a little while." I had to give that woman credit for perception and tact. With the promise of food, D.J. cheerfully followed her down the hall to the back of the house. I had no excuse to put off the call, much as I wanted to forget I even had an ex-husband. I clenched my teeth as I dialed his number.

"Hi, David."

"It's about time you got back to me. I called twice." Had his voice always had this peevish undertone?

"We've been pretty busy." I was proud of the even tone I mustered in reply.

"So you've changed addresses? Again?"

"That's right," I bit back, clasping the banister and sinking to a nearby step.

"For Christ's sake, Mary Catherine, when's this going to end?" I held the phone farther away from my ear during the tirade, but stopped short of ending the call, congratulating myself on my powers of restraint.

"When's what going to end, David? The moving? Your infidelity? My hope for a fulfilling life?" Well, so much for restraint. His stony silence lasted so long I thought I'd lost service.

"This isn't all about you, you know. Not every damn thing is about you." Well, that was a revelation. And here all those years that I'd worked at a thankless job, run the household, placated him, pampered him, and raised his child, I'd thought it was all about me. Live and learn.

I took a deep breath. "D.J. seems happy with the new place. He has his own room. And there's a cat." I knew the cat would get to him.

"You got him a fucking cat? You know how I hate cats. He can't have a cat here."

"In case you haven't noticed, our son is with me. And besides, I didn't *get* him a cat. There's one that lives on the premises." I couldn't resist poking just a bit more. "D.J. really seems to love having a pet." I hadn't actually seen him interacting with Penrod, but I'm not above embellishing when the occasion calls for it.

"But a cat? A vicious, bird-killing cat?"

"It's a very friendly cat, David," I prodded. "It follows us around."

"Yeah, they all seem nice at first, till the claws come out. Remember *Pet Sematary*?"

"Some of us understand the difference between fiction and reality," I pointed out. "But, hey, maybe when you spend your life living a lie, you kind of lose that ability."

"I'm not going to listen to this."

"Good. Then I can hang up with a clear conscience. Just send the check."

"Have D.J. call me."

I smothered a sigh. "Will do." After ending the call, I reviewed my performance. Keeping my temper? C-minus. Standing my ground? A-plus. All together, I was above average. I'd made adequate progress.

"Progress, Penrod." The cat's unblinking stare from the landing cast me into doubt. Who was I kidding? Obviously neither of us.

When in doubt, I find food offers clarity. I suppose that accounts for my pants size. I didn't spare the dark corners more than a glance as I crossed the carpets through the hall and dining room to the back of the house. The enticing tang of onions, tomato, and garlic combined with the unmistakable smell of cooked hamburger made me realize that I hadn't eaten in hours — another sign of change. One thing that didn't change was D.J.'s appetite. My kid's the Pasta King, a true connoisseur of all things starchy. He needed two hands to lug his serving to the counter where a stool waited. Mrs. Parrish was nowhere in sight.

"Looks like that mess should hold you for a while." I ruffled his golden mane just to annoy him.

"More where this came from. I made it myself." Years of practice let me translate the words that filtered through spaghetti strands.

"Plates?"

"Over there." He nodded to a bank of cabinets that housed enough china for a state dinner. I tugged a dinner plate from a stack and filled it, rationalizing the calories I must've burned going up and down the stairs with all those boxes.

"Mmm. Good as always, kiddo." I gave the sauce the attention it deserved.

"Mrs. P. said she liked it too. She didn't want much, though."

"So where is she?" I wondered whether the help was expected to always eat in the kitchen—a detail that hadn't occurred to me until now.

"She said she needed to check on something upstairs."

Unbidden, a ghastly picture-postcard of the thing in the bed popped into my head. I wondered if Aunt Beatrice needed to be tucked in for the night.

CHAPTER FIVE

Actively investigating and debunking paranormal phenomena since 2008, the Paranormal Posse is dedicated to shedding daylight on the shadowy world of the supernatural. Since the team began its investigations, it has examined over 200 cases in Pennsylvania, New Jersey, and Delaware, applying scientific techniques and cold common sense to prove there's nothing in the dark but...dark.

"What are you watching, kid?" D.J. had left me alone with the smeared red dishes to retreat to his new room, where he was now hunched over his computer. The keyboard and monitor looked out of place among the walnut bureaus and Morris wallpaper. Sitting cross-legged on the hulking four-poster bed, he looked disconcertingly young and vulnerable.

"An episode of *Ghost Stalker*. You know, Mom, that show where the guys go in and use EVP and stuff to figure out why spirits are haunting some place?" I idly wondered what an EVP might be.

"The one with the former police detective and that snarky tech guy with the glasses?" I asked, brushing a hank of hair from his forehead, a gesture that earned an irritated shrug.

"No, that's *Paranormal Posse*. That's, like, totally different. Those guys go into supposedly haunted houses to prove it's all a lot of bullshit." He still didn't bother taking his eyes from the computer to answer.

"Don't say 'shit.'" My head was starting to ache.

"You say it." When he finally looked up, his beatific smile made my hand twitch.

"Only under duress." The mantle of good motherhood had obviously frayed, but I wasn't about it cast it off entirely.

"So what's this episode about?" I sat down next to him, bedsprings protesting.

"They're in this old mental hospital where the ghosts are retarded and don't know they're dead."

"Disabled. Or—differently abled." I might as well have saved my breath. He was lost in the spirit world.

"So they're going down this hallway near the place where some dentist pulled out all the teeth of patients who acted out, right? And this ghost comes and—"

"Did you actually see a ghost?"

"Well, you see the guys say, 'What was that?' And then the camera shows the end of the hall where the ghost was." On the screen, the camera was panning wildly as the sound went to static.

"So you don't actually see—" I pressured.

"The guy with the tattoo said later that something grabbed his arm." He finally wrenched his gaze from the laptop to face me.

"Again, you don't actually see—"

"And there were scratches on it—like, five scratches all the way down his arm." Raising his own arm, D.J. traced a replica of the claw marks. I suppressed a shudder at the theatrics.

"Remember that word I told you not to say? This would be an appropriate context." I hugged his arm to my side. "No such thing as ghosts, kiddo."

"Bet that's what the Ghost Stalker used to think too," he leered, "until they reached from beyond the grave for him." His sardonic cackle would've been more effective if his voice hadn't cracked.

"I think I must be more the *Paranormal Posse* type." I rubbed his back. "You're going to get a sore neck bending over the computer like this. And you must be pretty tired. Let's get your bed made up." When I pulled back the chenille spread, I was surprised to see fresh sheets. "Who—"

D.J. waggled his brows. "Must be friendly ghosts. Come on, Mom. It's way too early for bed." He bent down, typing in a new site. "Look, I'll download a *Posse* episode."

The opening screen flashed names and pictures of Peter Larsson, Head Investigator with 15 years' experience on the Philadelphia police force, and Anthony Proforta, Tech Expert and Science Officer. Tony looked a lot like my junior high English teacher: short, dark, round, and intense, with a glint in his eyes behind the black frames. Peter looked more like a displaced Viking—tall, blond, stiff-jawed, and bored. No wonder ghosts fled when they arrived. I wouldn't open the door to either of them.

The Viking's voice was just as bored as his expression. *Today we are standing outside of this unassuming three-bedroom ranch in New Jersey. As you can see, it looks like every other house in this middle-class subdivision. And we're here to prove it is, despite the claims of the renters who are seeking to get their security deposit back because it's, yes, you guessed it, haunted. Tony, fill us in on the backstory.*

The camera shifted from the flat line of the chiseled mouth to a place that reminded me of our former rental—nondescript and a little ratty. A new voice, deep and tough with the distinctive flat twang of South Philly, came through in voice-over.

Peter, this is the rented home of Raven and Raphael DeCosta, though they refuse to live in it. The landlord, Michael Bond, says they're just deadbeats trying to weasel out of paying rent and hoping to get their faces on T.V. The DeCostas moved out in March, and their case has been in the courts ever since.

An attorney we consulted says that this isn't the first case of its kind, believe it or not.

The screen flashed a picture of a rambling Victorian monstrosity. *Back in the 1990s, some folks in New York bought a — as they termed it — 'haunted' house and then learned from the locals of its disturbing history. The buyers sued and actually won their case against the sellers, who not only knew about the house's rep but even sold the story to the media.* The camera cut to a lurid tabloid article. *Here's the thing, though, Peter. The buyers didn't actually have to prove the place was haunted. They just had to prove the sellers knew about the rumor.*

The camera cut to Peter. *So Tony, if I hear you right, no one proved there were ghosts?*

The disembodied voice of Tony answered, punctuating each word. *No, Peter, no one even tried. Because, as we know, there's no such thing as ghosts.*

I was distracted from Tony's testimony by a noise in the hallway. Something was tapping — random and faint, but insistent.

"Turn up the volume, will you?" I said, propping a pillow behind my head and stretching out. "I'm having trouble hearing."

D.J. looked over his shoulder and grinned. "Addictive, huh? Wait'll they start in on the interviews, Mom. That's the best part." D.J. scooted back against the headboard, settling the laptop between us. On screen, the bloodless, imperious Peter dominated the DeCostas, who were understandably cowed. To the couple's right hovered a wraithlike woman whose pasty features stood out against her black shirt. When the camera shifted to a close-up, a caption identified her as *Sylvie Blakely, Purported Medium*. She was explaining to a visibly sneering Peter that she served as a translator. Other times, she was a temporary vessel — an intermediary for spirit entities who desire to project their essences from the Other Plane to this one. It all sounded kind of messy to me, like somebody would have to mop up the ectoplasm with a pine cleaner when they were finished.

The most unaffected of the bunch was a huge German shepherd that wandered in and out of frame, oblivious to both camera and supposed entities. Named, unaccountably, Skippy, he played the part of the Posse's mascot. The moment he sniffed Peter's crotch was golden. I immediately became a Skippy fan.

"You know, Mom, the new season's starting soon, and they're going to be investigating, like, just a couple towns over, in Radnor and Merion. 'Haunted Hoaxes of the Main Line' or something. And you can even nominate your favorite ghostly mansion." I could see the tiny neurons sparking in his addled brain and stepped in to short circuit that impulse.

"D.J., you wouldn't..." The knocking was louder now — and centered directly on D.J.'s door.

CHAPTER SIX

I couldn't ignore this knock, especially since it was accompanied by a quavering voice. "Mrs. Livingston? Are you there?" Mrs. Parrish sounded breathless. Guilt sent me bouncing off the bed and opening the door. She looked shorter than before, more insubstantial, perhaps wilting with fatigue from scaling those steps and trekking down the hall. I was grateful to see she must have turned the lights on, because behind her a wall sconce cast a yellow glow.

"Did you need something, Mrs. Parrish?" I pulled the door wide and looked to the far end of the corridor, where Aunt Beatrice's door remained closed. I hadn't realized my shoulders were tense until I felt them relax. "Would you like me to make some decaf coffee or a pot of tea, or —" Since my knowledge of a companion's role was largely gleaned from novels, I really had no idea what duties I may have neglected. Come to think of it, though, a pot of tea sounded damn good.

"Well, that would be lovely, but I just came by to outline a schedule for Saturday. I'm so eager to get started, you know." She perched on the armchair near the door, blue-veined hands fluttering like moths. "All those notes and snapshots. Given your background, I just know you're the ideal person to help me organize them." The woman's intensity was a little alarming.

"Of course, I'm happy to help in any way that I can," I responded automatically, while in the background I could hear the computer emit a deep-throated howl. The voices of Tony Proforta and Mrs. Parrish erupted in unison.

"What was that?" The howl cut off when D.J. shut the computer, laughing. Glaring at him over my glasses, I waited until he straightened up before answering.

"We were just watching a video together," I said, stepping between her and my still snickering son. "It's wonderful to have a high-speed connection here." D.J. had crowed over it when he'd set up his toys earlier in the day, marveling at the quickness of his downloads — so much better than the signal he had been tapping into from an unidentified neighbor.

"How nice to see a mother and son who enjoy each other's company," she answered. At that, I'm sure D.J gagged, though I kept my eyes on Mrs. Parrish, who obviously hadn't tracked me down just for idle chat.

"So tomorrow," I prodded.

"Oh, yes, I'd like to get started early. I can think so much more clearly in the morning — mist rising, clear air, all the promises of a new day, you know."

In fact, I didn't know and had no desire to know what early morning air was like at Grey Crag. The last time I'd faced early morning in this state, I'd been in high school. Time had mercifully dulled that memory. Other memories I kept a lid on. With an effort, I dragged my attention back to my job description. "What time would you like to get started, Mrs. Parrish?"

She pursed her mouth as she considered. "Well, after breakfast and my morning exercise, certainly. Shall we say...seven?" She studied my face. "Or, uh, seven-thirty?"

I think I managed a reasonable facsimile of a smile. "Seven-thirty will be just right. I love a bracing start to the day." Behind me, D.J. snorted, but I held onto my smile as if my livelihood depended on it. "How about if I bring that pot of tea to the library and you can tell me a little more about your project?"

* * *

Fifteen minutes later, I balanced a tray heavy with a teapot, cups, saucers, and shortbread cookies imported from Scotland, no less. Six tins of them were lined up neatly in the butler's pantry. Setting the array on the mahogany table in front of the fireplace, I sank down next to my employer, who was already primly arranged on the brocade sofa. Gingerly, I poured tea into the porcelain cups (authentic Crown Derby — I'd seen the mark on the bottom). Mrs. Parrish spread a napkin across her lap and sighed happily. "Constant Comment?"

"My favorite," I admitted. Obviously, we shared a reverence for the beverage. "And good tea always tastes better in a china cup." So true.

"I think these were my grandmother's, or maybe her mother's. So hard to remember it all anymore." She shook her head. "That's why you're such a godsend. I need to get it all down before I go." She looked towards the alcove to her left, where a library table held an impressive pile of leather-bound volumes and scrapbooks. "A family history, you see."

"What a fascinating idea," I replied with what I thought was just the right touch of deference tinged with polite curiosity. "I'm sure your relatives will love having a record of their legacy."

"Oh, they surely will. Another way to live on, like the hospital wing or the pipe organ downtown." Her nod was emphatic. "They'll be very much in favor of it."

"And it's the kind of thing that they can pass on to future generations," I added.

Mrs. Parrish shifted and put down her cup. "Oh, well, that's out of the question, I'm afraid, Mrs. Livingston." She looked me in the eye. "You see, I'm the only one in the direct line still living."

CHAPTER SEVEN

Internet Results: *Dark Entities.*
We spiritual advisers are frequently asked this question. Entities, whether light or dark, like parasites, seek a suitable host — one with the requisite resonance and vibration. These dark entities are shadows not of people but of some other being. Their energy is negative. Like a virus, they attach themselves to a vulnerable victim. It is important to note that only the victim has the power to end the attack, if he or she can summon the necessary intestinal fortitude.

That night, I dreamt of Grey Crag. It seemed to me I waited at the base of the long drive, but I couldn't move, transfixed as I was by the distant stone façade, sharp-edged in the moonlight. Then, in the odd way of dreams, I was floating above a dirt track instead of a paved drive, following its languid turns over the lawn to the crest of the hill. There the mansion stood, not as I had seen it that first day, but as it must have been a hundred years before asphalt and autos marred the hills where now only the thin creak of crickets intruded. And as I watched, a shadow loomed in front of me.

"Mom, wake up."

I tunneled into the pillow, trying to recapture that sense of floating. "Go away."

43

D.J. wasn't about to give up that easily. "You wanted me to be sure you were out of bed by seven," he said, prodding again.

"That couldn't have been me. It must've been some cruel imposter." I groaned when D.J. pulled at the spread I had wound about my body. "Just a few more minutes," I mumbled, pulling back.

"You told me not to listen to you when you said that." His voice cut an irritating wedge in my stupor.

"I was in the middle of a great dream, and you ruined it." No longer floating, I let fragments of the day's schedule fight their way into my consciousness. Seven? I had to get to work.

"What was so great about it?" D.J. paused at the door. "Your dream, I mean."

I thought of the mysterious floating sensation and a sense of a time long gone. "Well, this morning, it just seems silly," I admitted, reaching for my glasses to help myself focus and knocking the dog-eared copy of *Rebecca* to the floor. "So what are you doing today?"

"What is there to do?" There was an edge to his voice that had me look up. "At home I could hang out with my friends. Here there's nobody. It sucks."

I thought of my friend Jodie and the talks we'd have over pie at the local café in our old neighborhood. He had a point. "Well . . . you could finish unpacking. Read a book. Pick up the clothes on your floor. Shower."

"Yeah, well, maybe you should consider that too. Your hair's, like, standing straight up." I shooed my son out, hobbled to the bathroom, and managed to clean up, drag on jeans and t-shirt, and slip into sandals with five minutes to spare. Sliding my hand down the polished banister, I speculated about the possibility of coffee. The landing was dark since sun didn't penetrate the west windows at this early hour. As I crossed below them, I felt something brush my scalp and send a tingle down my neck. *Spider web*, I thought. It had to be a spider web. Knowing I was being ridiculous, I still darted to the other side of the landing to avoid it.

I sped down the remaining stairs, turned to pass the entryway, and continued to the library, where the sunlight streaming through the bay windows of the alcove to my left blinded me for a few seconds. When my eyes adjusted, I realized Mrs. Parrish, perfectly groomed and energetically attired in a lavender cardigan, was already shuffling through the pile of books, pasting sticky notes to pages and humming to herself. It was going to be a long day.

The first caffeine-deprived hour went by in a haze while Mrs. Parrish chattered and I handed her more sticky notes. Together, we tagged a journal with a scrawled entry describing a christening, a scrapbook containing a newspaper clipping for a Huntsman's Ball, and an album that held a photograph of a white-haired patrician gentleman seated stiffly in a wicker chair, his index finger marking a page in a book, his gaze challenging the camera. "My father, James Craggun," Mrs. Parrish explained. "I think they buried him in that suit."

She took a phone call at eight, leaving me the opening I needed to brew a pot of dark Colombian and munch on a stray banana. From the open box of cereal, puddle of milk, and dirty bowl, I deduced D.J. had come and gone. At least he'd eaten. I wondered briefly if he had any plans for the day beyond eating more and hoped he let me know if he left the house. Otherwise, I'd never know, given the size of the place.

The hum of a vacuum drew me to the dining room, where a short young woman in a white uniform pushed an ancient Hoover. She looked up, startled, then tapped her toe on the lever to stop the machine. "You're the boy's mother," she said, grinning, her teeth bright against her caramel skin. "He doesn't look much like you."

I wondered what was so funny, but felt I had to own up to the relationship. "No, I mean, yes, I'm D.J.'s mom, um, Mrs. Parrish's new companion. Mary Catherine." When I held out my hand, she wiped her palm against her side before extending hers.

"Zina. D.J. and me, we met in the kitchen. *La madre que me parió*, he gave me a heart attack sneaking up like that. I just about wet myself." Her rich chuckle let me off the hook. She didn't seem mad.

"I'm sorry he surprised you. I'm sure he didn't know anyone else was here."

"Mrs. P. had me make up your rooms last week, so I knew you were coming." She unplugged the machine. "Nice to have a kid in the house for a change."

I looked into the drawing room behind her. "Do you have any idea where he's gone?" At this point, my maternal instinct was twanging like a taut rubber band.

Zina stopped looping the cord. "He asked me what there was to do around here. Told him there's not much except maybe the creek and pond down the road. He seemed real interested when I mentioned the old church though."

You hear people say their blood ran cold, but until then, I hadn't believed it could happen. Mine had ice chips floating in it. "The old Episcopal church?" I prayed I was wrong.

"That one right over the little bridge." Zina wheeled on in search of more unsucked carpet while I stayed stuck in the summer I was twelve.

* * *

We had started out after lunch, Amy, Carrie, Margaret, and I, intent on adventure. That June the branches hung heavy with leaves that bowed over us as we coasted our bikes down Waterloo Avenue, careening onto Sugartown Road and taking the first fork to wind past cool streams and thick shade, a welcome relief in the heavy summer heat. We stopped for a while to wade across a dam slippery with moss, then trap tadpoles, wiggling wet in our hands, their legs already sprouting. It was late afternoon when we wheeled past Grey Crag, frowning from its hill. Clouds were massing when we finally crossed the bridge under the cover of birches and leaned our bikes against the fieldstone barrier surrounding the church and its cemetery.

There, boxwood grew as tall as the arched church windows and gravestones butted against the walls, stretching like ragged teeth across the graveyard. Subdued at first, perhaps weighed down by the oppressive silence of the cedars, we tiptoed over bodies we imagined beneath our sneakers, thinking protruding roots were bones working their way to the surface.

Occasionally, we paused to read an epitaph, discovering an infant born and dead the same December day, marveling at a 90-year-old woman named Mehetabel, of all things, and tripping on headstones sunk so deep the moss had nearly covered them, leaving only the pocked white tops above the dark earth. The oldest grave we saw was dated 1748, though we knew some were older, and that a Revolutionary War general was also buried on the grounds. Carrie had a hiccup of hysteria when she saw her name, Carolyn L. Treadwell, with a death date of 1900.

Amy, my sometime friend and sometime foe from the moment we entered first grade together, had lost interest in history by this time and was itching for some action. "Come on, guys. This is boring. We should play hide-and-go-seek." Ordinarily, we'd think ourselves too mature for a grade school game, but twisted trees and lines of tombs promised untold thrills. "I'll count," Amy shouted, already running to hide her face against a weeping angel. "One, two…" Carrie and Margaret raced uphill to the section of newer graves, so I ran down the path where I saw a cluster of small buildings.

They were mausoleums with family names carved in block letters above the lintels and heavy iron grates barring doors and windows. I wondered, as I pulled at each door, why a house of the dead needed a window, but lost that thought when one grate, far more rusty than the rest, yielded to my tugging. Up the path, I heard Amy reach fifty, so I stepped in and pulled the grate behind me.

The smell of mildew burned my nose, and underneath that smell, another darker odor waited, one I can't name even decades later. Though dim inside, enough sun found its way through the window and door to let me see the skeletal remains of last fall's leaves scattered on the floor and tangles of webs shrouding the corners. The space was deeper than I'd imagined, with a wall of brass plaques opposite the door. No light reached as far as those corners.

Outside, the wind had picked up, sending leaves slapping and limbs waving to the incoming storm. Thunderstorms in June roil quickly, the only warning a zip of ozone in the air before the cracks and snarls take over. Rain descended that afternoon like grey sheets, forcing me to choose between drenching and musty darkness. All the warmth had been siphoned from the day, and the marble at my back deepened the chill. But I was dry, while Margaret and Carrie were undoubtedly soaked beneath funereal cypresses, and Amy, who had stopped counting, probably found only cold comfort beneath the angel's wings.

They say they found me when the storm blew over, having searched sanctuary and paths for an hour. They found me, squatting there, unmoving, eyes open. And when they coaxed me up and drew me into the fading sunset, they saw the bruise above my elbow, the bruise with four impressions, just like fingers.

.

CHAPTER EIGHT

"Mrs. Livingston, I'm off the phone now, if you'd like to come back." Mrs. Parrish had to repeat the invitation before I followed her to the library, leaving behind a coffee cup and a sense of dread. D.J. had a good head on his shoulders, I reminded myself. He was resourceful and mature for his age. Besides, he wasn't the sensitive type. Nothing would happen to him in the graveyard.

Mrs. Parrish's enthusiasm hadn't waned. She pawed happily through a cardboard box, straining to decipher the faded writing on the back of each photograph. "Mrs. Livingston, can you make this one out? I believe it's a picture of my cousin's girl, Lainie Barnhart, at the Philadelphia Charity Ball, but I can't quite tell what this date is, which would help me be sure." She handed the photo to me.

"I think it's 1985," I told her. The hairstyles looked more like 1962, but the Main Line had never been what I'd consider fashion forward—not that I was one to talk, I reminded myself. I hiked up my sagging jeans and tugged down the faded college T-shirt that stretched thin across my chest. First paycheck, I'd hit the mall.

"That early? Oh, it's not Lainie, then," Mrs. Parrish replied. "I wonder who it is." She looked at the picture as if waiting for it to speak, then set it aside.

"This must be an amazing party," I marveled, picking up the photo and admiring the smattering of ingénues in white and their escorts in black, like a flock of doves chained down by penguins. Everything was larger than life. It could be the set for a period film.

"Oh, it is. The Charity Ball's been held every year since the 1880s, you know. And it starts off the season." Mrs. Parrish practically gushed as she described the year's haute events. I felt like I was stuck in the middle of a Regency novel without a glossary to guide me, but since she was geared up now, I had to wait her out. "Of course, I prefer the Red Ball in March. The food's so much better," she concluded.

Well, that I could relate to. "Every party's better with good food," I replied.

Her eyes lit up. "That reminds me. The Union League's annual luncheon and fashion show is coming up. I should have put it in my engagement calendar. I hear several of the ladies are wearing hats this year," she positively twittered. "And Mrs. Donald Haynes is singing the National Anthem!" Though I was underwhelmed at the prospect, I made appropriate listening noises while continuing to sort pictures into piles by event — gala, holiday, European tour.

In fact, I was fascinated by the proof of how these people spent their time. They seemed to do everything imaginable except work. Old sepia photos showed couples lounging on the veranda of the Croft Hall Hotel in Ocean City. On the vast lawn of the Merion Cricket Club, men in white shorts and shirts played croquet. Big-hatted women mugged from the powder blue grandstand at the Devon Horse Show. The pictures raised yet more questions. Where did they buy those shorts? What was this pervasive interest in hats? Were wealthy matrons prone to hair loss?

A bang and clatter from the entryway made us both look up. I hoped the sound meant that D.J. had found his way back from whatever trouble he'd uprooted, but it was Zina, wrestling with a floor polisher that must have weighed as much as she did. The distinctive smell of Johnson Paste Wax brought me back to my girlhood, hours spent buffing the dining room table while my mother smoked a Tareyton and pointed out spots that I'd missed.

"Will this bother you ladies?" Zina asked, already reaching to plug the behemoth into the outlet near the door. "I don't know how this floor gets so bad so fast," she muttered to herself. I kept my mouth shut, but I knew the answer to the mystery. The night before, I'd caught D.J. testing how far he could slide down the hall with a hefty running start. He'd developed enough momentum to make it halfway to the drawing room before I put a stop to it, unwilling to see the contents of the urn on the mantel dusting the parquet. Every party needs a party pooper.

As if on cue, my progeny appeared in the doorway, a swampy stench and squelch surrounding him like an aura. With every step he took, he left a soggy Converse print behind. *He'd picked the duck pond after all*, I thought in relief as I crossed towards him, checking for cuts, bruises, and possible leeches. Of course, he backed away from the motherly inspection. When I reminded him he was my only child and thus was required to submit to the ministrations, he treated me to the same look that Possessed Regan gave her mother in *The Exorcist*. How sharper than a serpent's tooth it is...

From her expression, I expected Zina would speak up as my boy tracked across her newly polished wood, and she did, shutting off the machine to lash into him, her diatribe laced with Spanish. D.J., who grew up where signs are bilingual, answered her cheekily in kind, and by the end of their sparring, both were laughing. I didn't pick up much of it since my understanding of the language is limited to the years I spent quizzing him for tests. I'd taken twelve years of French, which proved useful only on my honeymoon and the rare times David took me to a nice restaurant. Ah, *c'est la vie*.

Merde. David. It was Saturday, and I had promised to call with an update. At least I'd be able to report that his son was safe and sound for now. I walked past Zina and D.J. onto the covered portico so no one would overhear. The conversation was likely to be difficult.

"Hi, David."

"I've been waiting for you to call me." Only David can instill guilt from four hundred miles away.

"Been a busy morning." I padded down the stone steps and stood gazing at the leering gargoyle above me. Just now, I thought the creature bore a remarkable resemblance to my ex-husband.

"So I gathered. I talked to D.J." That was a leading question if ever I heard one. My force field went up.

"He called you?"

"Earlier. He doesn't sound happy, Mary Catherine."

"He's a teenage boy, David. They never sound happy. It's the hormones."

"Do I need to come up there?" The threat was implicit. I felt it to my bones.

"Oh, stop it, David. He's fine—just taking a little while to adjust to a new place. Once he starts school, things will be better for him." I hoped. The line went quiet. "David? Are you still there?"

"It's not the same here now." His voice was muffled and distant.

"I imagine not." On a Saturday, we'd usually be shopping or watching D.J.'s soccer match or working on the yard.

"Remember what we used to do early Saturday mornings?"

I remembered all too well. That's how we got D.J. "Yeah. Best day of the week." Now the gargoyle looked nothing like David. And the day had warmed up. I tugged at the collar of my shirt, which felt very tight.

"We could have that again, Mary Catherine." I had to admit it was tempting. He'd caught me off guard with my defenses down.

"What about needing space?" I had heard all about it—his need for space and more options, my nonstop demands, the way I failed to fully appreciate how much he did.

"It's empty," he said, and I felt the pain and effort behind the words.

"David, you made your choice, and I made mine." Inside, I saw Zina cross the hall and peer out at me. "Listen, can we talk about this later? D.J. just got back from playing outside, and he's covered in muck, and we haven't had lunch yet." I ended the call before he had a chance to answer, and for extra measure, I turned off the phone before reentering the house. Zina still hovered about the entryway.

"I told D.J. to go clean up that mud," she said. She looked at the phone in my hand. "That D.J.'s father?"

So much for personal distance. I didn't see any point in brushing her off. "Yeah. He likes to check in to see how things are going."

She stood in the shadow of the doorway, considering me. "The boy looks like him, yes?"

"Yes. David's very tall and fair."

"Pretty like your boy, huh?"

"Yes. He's very good looking." I smiled slightly, remembering.

"How you get a man like that?"

CHAPTER NINE

Posse Protocol:
1. Confirm the client's request with a phone interview (P.I.)
2. Assess the site with an overall occult preliminary site investigation and evaluation
(O.O.P.S.I.E.)
3. Conduct on-site interviews (O.I.)
4. Conduct a scientific overview of site (S.O.S.)
5. Analyze data gathered (D.A.)
6. Report investigation parameters (R.I.P).

If a pod of aliens had stood at the door when I yanked it open, I couldn't have been more surprised. There I swayed, barefoot, in black yoga pants and an old white T-shirt of D.J.'s, face to face with a video camera and crew. Aliens would've been more welcome.

Mrs. Parrish had already left with her designated driver for some pre-luncheon festivities and the much-anticipated fashion show, and D.J. was doing what a teen does best, sleeping. Now that I'd settled in, Zina had stopped coming in on weekends. I'd regarded the free morning spread out before me as mine to bask in, poking about the house, unpacking a few more boxes, reading a novel, maybe even painting my toenails. After days of navigating Grey Crag's convoluted past, I anticipated savoring the open hours in countless ways. Not one of them was now smiling expectantly at me on the doorstep. Catching a glimpse of myself reflected in the lens facing me, I tucked my loose hair behind my ear, pushed my glasses up my nose, and crossed my arms in front of my braless chest, all the while trying to stay in the shadows.

"Mrs. Parrish?" God, how old did I look? The commanding voice from the back of the herd stepped forward, followed by a wagging police dog. Once I registered those finely carved features and those broad shoulders, that lolling tongue and eager nose, I started closing the door. "I'm afraid Mrs. Parrish isn't in right now. You'll have to try later this afternoon." Surely she'd be back by then. If not, I could just pretend I didn't hear the chimes.

"No problem, people," the man blocking the door boomed to his underlings. He looked even more imposing up close than he had on D.J.'s computer screen. Yes, it was Peter Larsson and his posse, in person—and canine. "She said to just make ourselves at home if she was out." He waved them forward. "In we go." Larsson and the stampede of six pressed past me and jumbled into the entryway, jostling a vase and maneuvering me into a corner, literally and figuratively. Standing a few steps below the landing like he was holding court, Peter positioned himself above the fray, with Skippy standing guard next to him. Thankfully, Penrod was nowhere to be seen.

The milling herd cut me off from the land line, and my cell phone was upstairs, so I couldn't call 911. Obviously, I had to fall back on my resources. I summoned my Teacher Voice, reserved for moments like this, when the world veers sideways. "Yo. You there scratching the paneling. Cut it out.

Right now." I added the infamous intimidating glare over my glasses. "You heard me." My volume crescendoed until every mouth gaped. Well, almost—Peter the Great just thinned his lips, but he did stop giving orders and even looked a tad sheepish. Skippy, however, didn't seem impressed. "I don't know where you think you got the right to barge in here, mister, but you and your entourage can start barging back out right now." I had the satisfaction of seeing the posse freeze, all jostling suspended. But before I could press my advantage, I heard that fatal sound from the stairway.

"Oh, cool!" D.J. stood on the landing, bathed in colored light, enthralled by the mess in the entryway. "They came. They really came." My scalp prickled with suspicion, honed by fourteen years of trying to corral this kid. Something was rotten in the state of Pennsylvania, and I suspected it was my offspring.

Pushing my way through the bodies, I mounted the steps to confront him. "Just what have you been up to?" Below us, the posse tuned in like an audience at a play.

D.J. was characteristically unfazed and devoid of any decent sense of guilt. "Well, you know how I told you about how the Paranormal Posse was going to do a show about places around here? And you could, like, nominate your favorite haunted house? And so when you first told me that we were moving here, I went online and found all sorts of stuff about Grey Crag, right? And about how it has this reputation and there used to be séances and weird sh—crap like that. And so I talked to Mrs. Parrish that day...and she was really interested and—"

"Do you mean that Mrs. Parrish actually invited these freaks into her home?" That prickling scalp was now a cold spike down my spine. He nodded, beaming. Below us, the posse grew restless. "Do not move. Not a muscle," I called

59

down. I ran to my room and grabbed my phone, dialing 411. "Philadelphia. Union League," I requested. Minutes passed before a disgruntled Mrs. Parrish came on the line.

"We were just about to find our seats, Mrs. Livingston. What is it?" I quickly explained the situation downstairs. My heart sank when I heard her reply. "How wonderful! I'll be back as soon as I can. I know I can rely on you to keep them entertained until I can return, dear."

If only I'd known, I'd have prepared for the invasion. I'd have strung garlic around the door frames and sprinkled salt on the window sills.

CHAPTER TEN

It was Peter Larsson himself that stopped me from committing belated infanticide. With composure intact and a gleam in his icy blue eyes, Peter stepped between me and my troublemaking son, who was too busy scratching Skippy's ears to notice my death glare. "Excuse me. I take it you're the caretaker or something. I think this will make everything clear." He held out a fax, which turned out to be a signed contract with Mrs. Parrish's neat Palmer script looping above the dotted line. She'd given him leave to roam the grounds and to film at will, which I took as a sign of incipient dementia.

I tried hard to concentrate while Larsson droned on, explaining his agreement with my employer and her assurances he'd have full access to Grey Crag and its inhabitants whenever he found it convenient. But my attention kept getting snagged as the crew spread out and muscled all sorts of odd machinery about the place, laughing and talking now that they sensed they had free reign again.

I tuned back in as Peter was explaining the unique appeal of our location. "See, the history of Grey Crag is what first attracted us. It's pretty rare to find a site other than a hotel with this many deaths on record. And our preliminary search turned up all sorts of hits on Internet cesspools like hauntedhouse.com and real.haunts. So many factors to consider in this case…" He looked like a hound eyeing a squirrel. "Just exactly the kind of legend we love to debunk." He took in the vaulted ceiling, carved moldings, marble fireplace, and finally, me, with a satisfied, proprietary air. "It just doesn't get any better than this, right, Tony?" Not surprisingly, I'd failed to notice the sidekick. He was short where Peter was tall, dark to Peter's fair, stocky to Peter's trim.

"You're Tony," I said. We were almost the same height.

He held out his hand. "Anthony Proforta. Technology and research support." The hand was surprisingly warm, and so was his smile. "And you must be Mrs. Livingston." Then he glanced down and his gaze kind of stuck that way. I'd forgotten about the thin t-shirt.

"So, um, what's the first step?" I asked, again crossing my arms across my plump chest, disappointing the tech guy and Peter. At that point, D.J. had maneuvered himself into the circle and was lapping up every word. "Give me that hoodie," I whispered fiercely. He looked at me as if I were crazy, but he yanked it off and handed it over.

"We're here for the OOPSIE," Peter was saying, his attention on the boxes being unloaded from the van parked in the drive.

"You're what?" I pulled the hoodie over my head and pushed up the sleeves.

"The Overall Occult Preliminary Site Investigation and Evaluation," Tony clarified, openly grinning now.

"You're kidding." Now I knew how Alice felt when the Cheshire Cat first talked to her. I guessed that made Peter the Mad Hatter.

"We take nothing about haunting seriously, Mrs. Livingston," Peter stated, deadpan. "That's the point of the show." He stepped closer, invading my personal space. The dog moved with him. "Now, if you'd be willing to take us around and point out the hot spots, or maybe I should say cold spots..." He paused at my blank look, but D.J. jumped in.

"Oh, man. This is so incredibly cool. I'm gonna be on TV."

"You're not filming us now, are you?" In alarm, I looked down the stairs, wishing I'd showered. A red light blinked from the nearest video camera. "Oh, God, turn that thing off." I reeled back. "You can't just film a person. I mean, I have to sign a release or something, don't I?" Peter made a slashing motion at his throat, and the camera light blinked to yellow.

"It would really help if you could show us around so we can get the lay of the land here," Tony said smoothly. "No cameras. Just an informal walk-through so we can see where to set up equipment."

I thought about my paycheck. "Well, I guess we could..." And that's all it took before I was steering the tour down hallways, through doorways, and up stairways. I led them from cellar to attic, peeking in rooms I hadn't even known existed. Most of them had been closed off. There were about 20 in all, eight of them bedrooms. D.J. bounced along behind us like a puppy, adding juicy tidbits he'd gleaned from the Internet.

"So this is the room. I bet you can still find the bloodstains if you look. 'Cause you can never really get rid of blood. You can still see it, like even after years, when you spray it with this special stuff." I hovered by the door of the dark bedroom along with a whimpering Skippy, determined not to see if D.J. was right. Though Peter looked annoyed by

63

the commentary, he did kneel to get a closer look at the floorboards. Tony stood to one side with a light meter making notes on a tablet. Whenever D.J. started winding down, Tony prodded him with more questions—asking about the original owner, the deaths in the house, what websites were most useful. He seemed pretty used to kids.

Having finally exhausted the gore quotient on the second floor, we headed for the front stairs, the dog in the lead. "And that's the place the lady hung herself, right?" D.J. called from the hallway. "When she found him dead?" It seemed there was a horror story around every corner of Grey Crag, gleefully documented by my son. None of the seamier tidbits regarding the place had escaped his search, not illicit affairs, sensational suicides, or botched burials. I supposed I should be proud. By the time our tour ended back in the entryway, the crew was breaking for lunch. Somehow, though, I'd lost my appetite.

* * *

D.J. continued to tag along as the crew set up equipment throughout the early afternoon. When I could retreat, I quickly showered and dressed in conservative grey slacks, cream blouse, and heather cardigan, wishing it were a little longer so that it covered my rear. Better equipped to battle the invaders, I tracked Peter and Tony to the small parlor Mrs. Parrish had designated for my private use. So much for privacy, I thought. Afternoon sun was streaming in, reaching all but the furthest corner.

"So who's the good boy? Are you the good boy? Are you? Huh?" The dog stared at the slice of cheese dangling from Peter's hand. "Did you want this? This cheese? The cheese in my hand? Yes?" Finally, unable to take any more, the beast lunged. I had to laugh. "Oh, there you are," Peter said, looking up from a box lunch and folder of papers spread out on a side table. He continued feeding every other bite to his slobbering dog. "Wondered where you disappeared to. We need to get some information from you to complete your file." He stared for a few seconds too long. Skippy never took his eyes off the lunch.

"I have a file?"

"We always investigate the backgrounds of all those living at the suspected haunted site. You'd be surprised how many owners themselves perpetrate fraud in these cases."

I really had no opinion one way or the other about that, so I sat, crossing my feet at the ankles, while Peter hiked in the desk chair so it stood within inches of mine. He looked even more flawless up close. And just my type, damn it. On guard, I armed my warheads. Tony shifted in his seat across the room, then went back to fiddling with something electronic.

"Mrs. Livingston, uh, may I call you Mary Kate?"

"Absolutely not," I said. Peter looked momentarily taken aback, and I had to stifle a laugh. I guess he just wasn't used to somebody telling him 'no'.

"Mrs. Parrish assured me of your cooperation." His eyes bored into me, shutting me up. "So Mrs. Livingston, I've been reading over your history."

"Really? I have a history? Dull reading, I imagine."

"Actually, I found it very interesting. Especially the events of that day in June." He held up a printout of a newspaper article. "This particular story's part of what brings us here."

I felt a chill, despite the sun. "There's nothing worth reading in that," I replied evenly.

"Now, I have to disagree with you there. A vandalized cemetery, a historic site at that, is no everyday occurrence." He sat back in his chair and tapped his pen on the papers in front of him. "It made the paper, after all. Crosses upside down. Stones overturned. Sarcophagus lids cracked." He looked up at me.

"I had nothing to do with that."

"Maybe your friends put you up to it? As a dare?" Peter leaned forward.

"I told you—"

"Because, Mary Kate, this looks like a pretty serious bid for attention, if you ask me."

My temper flared. "If you'd just listen—"

"And the way you avoided any consequences was really impressive." He read another headline: "Local girl hospitalized, catatonic in wake of graveyard vandalism." Peter leaned back in his chair. "It seems like the common denominator in these unusual occurrences is one person." He laid another clipping down. "This Bicentennial event at Valley Forge Park. All these earlier incidents with your mother." His gaze worked hard to pierce my shell. "You were alone when you found her, correct?"

My throat had clamped down, so I stayed silent.

"You didn't really want to lie about your involvement that day in June and in the following weeks, did you? You just saw it as your only option, after everything else that happened. You know, Mary Kate, in your shoes, I'd have acted exactly the same way." The empathy sat uneasily on his face. I sensed a sneer underneath. Skippy had long since stopped wagging. Flashing lights and the static crackle of the squad car radio surged back from the past when I'd hoped to keep the memories six feet under. I was twelve again, paralyzed by the scrutiny and scorn of the local cops.

But I *wasn't* twelve anymore. I'd suffered this kind of manipulation all those years ago, but I was a big girl now, wasn't I? I didn't have to listen meekly to baseless accusations. And that irritating nickname was the final impetus. "The name is Mary Catherine. And I need to go." As I hurried out, face burning, I could feel at least two pairs of eyes following me.

In the hall, I ran right into a fluttery Mrs. Parrish. "Oh, Mrs. Livingston, isn't this exciting? When that nice Mr. Larsson phoned a few weeks ago, I had no idea he'd be here so soon." She stepped past me. "Hello, gentlemen. I do so hope Mrs. Livingston has made you feel at home. I must apologize for not being here to welcome you earlier." The woman practically vibrated in ecstasy. I felt Peter step behind me.

"We were just finishing up with Mrs. Livingston's interview," he said smoothly. "A few more questions." He put an unwelcome hand on my elbow to drag me back.

"Oh, please go on," my employer said. "I wouldn't dream of getting in the way of your investigation. This is such a wonderful opportunity!" I was trapped.

While I considered the best escape route, Tony came up, clipboard in hand. "Peter, how about I finish up the interview questions and get the forms filled out while you go ahead and meet with Mrs. Parrish? Maybe get a look at the grounds?" he said amiably. The tension slackened, and a placated Peter escorted Mrs. Parrish and Skippy out of the room. I could breathe again.

Tony's mouth twitched. "I promise to make it as painless as possible," he said, gesturing towards the back parlor. "Shall we?" I figured he must be taking the role of the good cop. After I sank into an armchair facing the table, he handed me the clipboard along with a pencil, all business.

Tony. The name suited him, I thought — straightforward, approachable. Not like that dick Peter.

Tony lumbered around the table where my file lay exposed. "Mrs. Livingston, while you're filling out the consent form, I have a few more routine background questions to ask you, following up on the data my colleague has already collected." He plunked down in the ladderback chair, filling the seat, but not the height. He glanced over the pile of papers at the form I was completing. "Your full name is Mary Catherine Donavan Livingston, correct? Married?"

Impressed with his ability to read upside-down, I was a little slow in responding. "Single. Now." I squirmed in my seat, feeling awkward and vulnerable.

Tony looked up, appraising, and then looked back at the file, flipping the page before continuing. "Okay, single. So, Mrs. — Mary Catherine, how often do you watch ghost hunting shows? Frequently? Occasionally? Seldom?"

"Never," I stated. But that wasn't strictly true. "Well, I did see part of yours."

He sat up a little straighter. "Really?" He seemed genuinely surprised and even a little pleased. "What did you think?"

I smiled. "I liked your dog."

Nonplussed, he paused briefly then returned to the questionnaire. "Have you ever before participated in a professional paranormal investigation? If so, when and where?"

"Are you kidding? People do this more than once?"

He checked 'no' before continuing to read the boilerplate. *That's right; I can read upside down too.* "The remaining questions are designed to establish the personalities of the participants, giving us a sense of how people's mindsets might be affecting what they see. We've adapted these questions based on the guidelines followed by the

Paranormal Research Center in Durham. Just answer 'yes' or 'no.' First one. Does your mood fluctuate easily?"

I thought about the way David could make my blood pressure rise with an offhand comment. Or the way D.J. could get me to laugh when I was in the middle of scolding him. Or my recent scuffle with Peter Larsson. "Define 'easily.' I mean, that's a very subjective term."

He raised his eyebrows above his glasses frames. "Do you undergo several rapid changes in mood throughout the day?"

"How many do you consider several?" I countered. I realized I was skirting the issue, but I couldn't seem to stop myself. Who was he to put me under a microscope, anyway? What gave these guys the right? I'd obviously been wrong in casting him as the good cop.

I swear he stifled a sigh as he rubbed the back of his neck where the black hair curled over his collar. "I'll put you down for a 'yes.' Next one. Have your thoughts ever been so powerful that they're like a voice speaking to you?" Again he pinned me with a gaze that made me feel like a deer stalked by a wolf.

"I don't think I like where this is going," I replied, looking down to study the pattern in the carpet. "Next question, please." I wasn't about to be labeled a schizophrenic.

He took off his glasses to rub his eyes. They were a rich shade of brown, I noted, like hot chocolate drizzled with butterscotch, rimmed with lashes longer than mine. "All right, Mary Catherine. How about this one? Do you ever experience a feeling of dread or a sense of a vague threat for no apparent reason?"

"What mother of a teenager doesn't?" I didn't bother hiding my irritation as I stood up to look out the window, pointedly turning my back on him, despite the fact that my pants were a little tight. Outside, I watched as Skippy crouched on the previously pristine lawn while Peter approached with a plastic bag. That cheered me up some. Tony didn't say anything for a while.

"Um, do—do you often overindulge in food and drink?" he asked cautiously.

So much for my elevated mood. I wheeled around. "Look at me. What do you think?" I opened my sweater wide, challenging him, but Tony kept his cool. He leaned back in the chair, which protested at the pressure, and took his time looking over the evidence before writing down a response. When I stretched to see the sheet, he covered the answer with his forearm. It was muscular and matted with black hair.

* * *

The next few questions probed in a number of areas I preferred to keep to myself—sense of confusion, frequency of daydreams, distractibility, self-image, impulse control, sociability. I tiptoed my way through them, alert to any changes in Tony's reaction.

"Last question." The corner of his mouth turned up. "And I promise it's really in the questionnaire. But I admit I'd like to hear your answer." He looked down at the clipboard. "Do you like to have your back massaged?" He kept his expression perfectly neutral, a technician to his heartless core.

I stared at him for a full five seconds. He gave nothing away. "That kind of depends on the circumstances." He waited me out, motionless, until I continued. "But with someone…" I could feel the flush rising. How long had it been since I'd felt someone's hands on my bare back? "Under the right circumstances…" I drew it out. "I very much enjoy being…rubbed."

"I see." With the table still between us, I couldn't tell if I'd gotten a rise out of him. But I knew I'd scored a hit.

70

Chapter Eleven

The first Ouija boards were supposedly made from coffin planks, and a coffin nail served as the planchette's pointer.

Read and Consider Before Operating the Online Ouija Board:

—Never play alone!

—Respect the spirits.

—Always "close" the board properly at the end of your session.

—Never let the spirits count down through the numbers or go through the alphabet.

—Never use the board in a graveyard or a place where violent death has occurred.

—Use with caution. (On March 20, 1920, police in El Cerrito, California, arrested seven when they "went mad" after consulting a Ouija board. Among those afflicted was a naked fifteen-year-old girl who explained she was better able to communicate with the spirits that way. The naked hysteria spread...)

Back in control, I walked out, hips swaying. Behind me, I heard Tony clear his throat, but I didn't bother looking back. The interview was over as far as I was concerned. In the hall I hopped over cables, dodged a man hugging a computer monitor, sidled past Penrod, now perched on a step, and skirted two women by the open door. One was young and bouncy, the other dark and sepulchral with a complexion like wax and eyes like empty sockets, her inky hair clinging to her skull. Yes, her I recognized: Sylvia something, the medium, dressed in the same tight black jeans and boots she'd worn for the last episode of *Paranormal Posse* I'd watched with D.J.

Usually I have no trouble blending into the woodwork, but the stars had aligned against me all day. Unidentified Bouncy Babe looked up as I tried to slip past. "Oh, here she is now. Ms. Livingston? Could you stop a minute?"

Did I really have a choice now that I knew Mrs. Parrish regarded the whole bunch as honored guests? Through the door I could see her pointing out the artful shrubbery to Peter. Accepting the inevitable, I stopped and pasted a polite smile on my face, all the while listening for noises from the parlor, hoping, hoping, hoping that Tony stayed put. "What can I do for you, Miss, uh …?"

"Ashley," she supplied. "I'm Mr. Larsson's production assistant. You know, sort of the go-to person, the one who does whatever the guys want."

I could just imagine. Then I thought of my current bank balance and reminded myself to be nice. "Do you need something, Ashley?" There, that was nice. I congratulated myself.

"I just wanted to introduce you to Sylvie Blakely. *The* Sylvie Blakely," she confided, leaning towards me. "The one who wrote *I See Dead People*? She really wants to meet you." Ashley was nearly overcome at the notion. I, however, was nearly overcome with the need to escape to the kitchen for sustenance and a restorative beverage — even more because I sensed Tony a few feet behind me now.

"How nice to meet you, Ms. Blakely," I said, extending my hand reluctantly. She took it in hers and held it long enough to make me wonder about her sexual orientation. I tugged, first gently and then forcefully, nearly backing into Tony, who'd closed the gap. "Um, was there a reason you needed to speak with me?" At that point, my mind had wandered longingly to that row of shortbread cookies in the pantry. Why couldn't these people leave me alone?

"Molly-Cat," Sylvie replied in a husky voice, "Stop the whining and get over it."

I froze. Then I was sick—suddenly, horrifically, gut-wrenchingly sick. I backed away from that voice, backed into the solid contours of the man behind me, shoved blindly at the hands that tried to steady me, and lurched around the corner towards the powder room. I heard only the rushing in my ears and felt myself cringing in anticipation.

Desperate, I shut the powder room door and leaned against it, heaving, cold sweat dotting my forehead. Eyes like pewter plates stared back at me in the mirror over the sink—the same grey eyes as hers. And that voice from Sylvie's mouth, the same voice, rough from smoking. The same mocking name, one I hadn't heard for decades. My mother's voice.

I don't know how long I stood in that bathroom before I pulled myself together enough to react to the knocking. It was Tony. He'd escalated to pounding before I shouted back that I was fine—just a little queasy from the heat. I was lying, of course. I felt cold all over, pale and shaking, incapable of repressing the whimpers. I leaned over the sink to slap water on my face, remembering how she used to hold my head below the faucet to drown the sobs.

* * *

I hadn't heard the door open, but I felt the draft and the hand on my shoulder. As that hand rubbed warm circles on my back, I stopped shaking and gradually released the edge of the sink. Tony reached his arm around me and turned off the water.

"Better now? "He watched my reflection carefully. My sanity trickled back, and along with it, intense embarrassment. I couldn't let anyone see me like this. After wiping my face with the hand towel, I took my time folding it neatly. I'd folded it twice before I could again meet his eyes.

"I—I'm fine. It was just so hot and close so—" I knew I was babbling. I hated this forced intimacy, this exposure. Unable to get a grip, I shivered again and crossed my arms, hugging them close.

"You seem cold, Mrs. Livingston," he said in the same gentle tone.

"Cold. Yes." I nodded stiffly.

"Let's find something warm to drink. The kitchen's down this way, isn't it?" He slipped an arm around my waist, pulling me from the sink. I resisted. "Come on, Mary." He walked me down the corridor, keeping up his aimless talk, until I found myself at the kitchen counter with my hands curled around a mug of hot tea.

He made orange pekoe, I thought idly. A solid black tea—no frills. The warmth from the tea spread, seeped from my hands to my mouth and through me. Long minutes passed before I could finally salvage something of my dignity, which was hanging in tatters right now, leaving me naked and vulnerable. "Thanks for the tea," I said, casting around for something—any topic—to distract us from the situation. "Aren't you having any?"

Tony shook his head. I played with the spoon, uncomfortable under his scrutiny. "Must be close to dinnertime by now," I added. That earned a nod, but his attention remained concentrated as he watched me drink. It wasn't until we heard the rumble of voices in the hall that he looked away.

"Need GPS to find your way through this place," Peter grumbled as he and Skippy strolled over to the counter, both skewering me with a look. "You about ready to close shop for the day, Tony? The old lady's off to some previous engagement. We can leave the equipment for now."

Tony stood. "Just have to grab some papers, round up the crew, and then we can head out." He paused at my side. "Take care, Mrs. Livingston. We'll be in touch."

The mug had cooled by the time I roused enough to order a pizza and make a salad. When I found myself tearing the lettuce into smaller and smaller pieces, I stepped back and forced myself down the hall, turning on lights as I went. On the landing, I called for D.J., who shouted back from his room. I took my time walking towards him, following his voice. "Pizza'll be here in a few," I said, trying to sound as normal as possible. As usual, he was glued to the laptop. "What'cha up to?"

"Found a new game. Want to see?" He lifted the computer.

"Maybe later. Got to grab my purse to pay the delivery guy. Why don't you bring it down with you?" The chimes were sounding when I made my way back downstairs, and I had plates and napkins arranged by the time D.J. appeared in the kitchen with the laptop tucked under his arm. I'd ordered extra cheese and black olives, his favorite, so he wasted no time digging in and chowing down two slices before he came up for air. I pushed the salad his way and made sure he ate some before I let him finish off the rest of the pie. I wasn't hungry.

"So you wanna see the game?" he asked, opening the laptop and powering it up.

"Sure." It was the best offer I was getting that night. "What kind of game is it?"

"Here. Check it out." The screen was black, but soon, a faint image swirled across the surface, gradually resolving into the outline of a cloaked figure holding a sickle. "Just click on it. On that box. The one that says 'click here.'"

A double click brought up an orange and black screen and released the sound of a creaking door. *"Read this before you dare to enter,"* the wavy banner announced.

"Go ahead and skip that, Mom," D.J. said impatiently. "Go to the next screen." I recognized the next image, the sun and moon and alphabet. It was a Ouija board, pointer hovering at its center.

The sense of cold returned. "This isn't a game, kiddo." He pretended not to hear me.

"So you use the mouse to operate the pointer thing and spell out your questions, right? And then it moves by itself to spell out the answers. Cool, huh?" D.J.'s eyes were fixed on the screen, his hand already moving the mouse.

I didn't say anything, mesmerized by the planchette pointer circling on the electronic board.

"So I ask it, like, a standard first question, right?" D.J. pulled the planchette across the alphabet to spell out the message: *"Is there anybody here?"* The monitor blinked and planchette wavered a moment, thinking. Then it began to move across the screen.

I slammed the computer shut, barely missing D.J.'s fingers.

CHAPTER TWELVE

Ironically, Labor Day at Grey Crag was filled with work—moving cartons and papers from one side of the library to the other, arranging piles into patterns only Mrs. Parrish seemed to follow. As I rummaged and she directed, she filled the quiet with family narratives—how her grandfather had hired the best Philadelphia architect of the time to build his retreat, how the stone had been quarried in Chester and brought to the rise 450 feet above the surrounding fields, 70-some acres of it theirs, much of the grounds kept wild for foxhunting. Then those lands had sounded with pounding hooves, flashes of red, and the full cry of hounds. To me it seemed her youth had been one unending house party where Biddles and Drexels mingled and gossiped and danced. She told of balls with black tie and boots themes that she and her Matthew had held, and of Beatrice's wedding in the main hall—the talk of the season.

One story captured my attention more than the rest: an event in the 1920s, when the spiritualism craze hadn't yet petered out before the specter of the Great Depression. "My aunt told me this story, you understand. It's not something my parents would mention." Mrs. Parrish looked blankly at the wall, staring into her past. "She'd tell me delicious little tidbits when I'd go to her room in the evenings and brush her beautiful dark brown hair. It was really quite magnificent, so long she could sit on it." She raised her arms to pat at her own short white curls.

"But this particular incident—it happened, Mrs. Livingston. And you can't unring a bell, can you?" I agreed, confused, and she continued. "You see, at that time, a science journal was offering a reward for proof of actual psychic ability. My mother was always looking for a new way to entertain, and on a lark, she organized a Halloween party. The idea was to call the bluff of a popular medium of the time. So on Halloween night, the guests arrived."

I could just imagine a crisp October night—ladies wrapped in velvet and brocade. Unwrapped, their bare arms and beaded gowns gleamed in the candlelight. The fast men among them, sporting trendy tuxedos and black ties instead of more sedate tails, smoked cigars. Ice tinkled in crystal tumblers that servers topped off with a steady flow of clandestine Canadian whiskey.

"They were laughing and joking, not taking it at all seriously, you see, even when they moved into the dining room for the session. But everything quieted down when the tabletop tilted early on." Mrs. Parrish paused for effect.

"That they could explain away, of course. But not the cold, so bitter they could see the fog of their breath. And the knocking was even harder to dismiss. Well, I suppose the medium could have rigged something to tap even if her hands were out where everybody could see them. But Mrs. Livingston, the tapping continued after the séance concluded. It went on into the night long after the last guest left." She smiled at my shiver. It was not a nice smile. "Needless to say, the family decided not to apply for the reward."

At that point, I retreated into the sunlight to get warm, needing a break from Mrs. Parrish and her peculiar house party. Someone must have been cutting grass. The green smell hung in the air. It was a sparkling day, the last of summer. I wished D.J. would come outside to enjoy it. I didn't like to think of him being swallowed up inside this house. He'd been moping about indoors, grousing about what he termed his last day of freedom before lockup. Back in the library, as I sorted and listened, half my mind remained on him. The other half stayed with the tale from the crypt told by batty Aunt Beatrice.

* * *

Tuesday, I drove my scowling son to his first day at the high school, a gleaming concrete building constructed years after I left the area. The new backpack hung heavy on his thin frame, even though so far the pockets held only spiral notebooks, pen, and calculator. I swallowed twice as I watched him lope through the glass doors without looking back and drove on only when the minivan behind me tapped its horn.

Buried in the library at Grey Crag, I kept busy throughout the morning transcribing notes from the string of Craggun narratives onto the computer, trying to make sense of the hodgepodge family history. Mrs. Parrish wanted every detail written down as if each act were invested in grave historical significance, which I suppose was the case, at least from her perspective. Her excitement over the project was touching, and she seemed unnaturally grateful for the minor effort I was making to preserve her heritage.

"So your grandfather was an officer of the Union League in the 1890s?" I entered the information on the timeline I was constructing in an effort to put the past in order.

"Yes, that's right," She nodded vigorously from her seat at the desk. "So was my father, and my husband's father, though that was a much later."

"Your father must've been fairly young when he married."

"Well, men matured so much faster then, I think, don't you?" She picked up a framed photo. "And with privilege comes responsibility. That's what he used to say."

"And what year did your father pass away, Mrs. Parrish?" Though I asked the question as delicately as I could, the woman shriveled before my eyes. This was obviously the wrong question.

"That was a very difficult time," she said. "You understand, I'm sure."

"I'm so sorry."

"The scandal, you know." She paused. "He used his pistol. The one he carried along on hunts." There were tears in her eyes at that point. "And when mother — "

"Why don't we stop for a while, Mrs. Parrish? We've been at this for hours." I was worried about the tremor in her hand as she lifted it to her face and her eyes withdrew somewhere I couldn't follow. "Mrs. Parrish?"

"Yes. All right. I think I'll go upstairs and lie down. Maybe you could bring something up for me later?" she asked, still staring at nothing. I had the uneasy feeling she was looking at the past that lingered, more real to her than the present. Whatever it was, the weight of it bent her over so that she seemed to have aged decades as she mounted the stairs.

I'd grown fond of her. She tolerated D.J. and gave me a flexible schedule so I could drive him to and from school. When the day's work was done, I'd often join her again in the library to share a cup of tea while I read out loud. To my delight, her tastes ran not to the untouched leather volumes on her shelves but to glossy, hardcover spy thrillers that she piled in a corner behind a wing chair. Sometimes she'd ask me to read a particularly grisly passage twice and then bemoan the thin crust of civility in the world.

She'd gotten under my skin, and I was beginning to feel somewhat protective of her.

After Mrs. Parrish took to her bed in the east wing, I had the afternoon to myself. Restless and surprisingly lonely, I poked around the files and papers until it was time to pick D.J. up from school. He grunted monosyllables in response to my questions until I gave up and we drove on in silence through town, down into the valley, and finally up the hill where the mansion waited, shrouded in the past with its doors firmly shut to intruders.

* * *

A more immediate past came to haunt me a couple of weeks later, when the unwelcome specters of Peter Larsson and Tony Proforta reappeared on the doorstep midmorning. Mrs. Parrish and I had just finished cataloguing the 1930s and were congratulating ourselves when we heard the van pull up, followed by Skippy's deep-throated bark. Zina let the men in without question, though Skippy was sent back outside to sit in the shade. I tried not to feel miffed. Skippy was the only one I cared to see. One look at Tony, and I felt embarrassed all over again.

Thankfully, the men sailed right past me this time, though Peter scanned Zina and me up and down as he and Tony strode across the room to Mrs. Parrish. Maybe he was looking for weapons. Tony didn't spare me more than a glance. That stung a bit.

I watched in disgust as the two of them set about cultivating my boss, drawing her out, flattering her. Within minutes Peter had himself seated by her side looking over the chronicle I'd been compiling. Tony took the other side, effectively bookending the old lady, who waved me off.

"Are you sure there's nothing more you need, Mrs. Parrish?" I said, looking pointedly at Peter.

"No, that will be all for now," she trilled. Well, I'd been dismissed like some parlor maid on a PBS drama. For the moment, I ranked with the shunned Skippy, who stared at me balefully through the window while Zina placed a mixing bowl of water on the grass next to him. At least Skippy got an ear scritch. I nursed my offended sensibilities all the way to my bedroom. Still sulking, I unpacked more boxes, finally leaving only one still full. I gave the last box a kick and flounced onto the double bed, which creaked at every movement.

With nothing to do, I was reduced to studying the wallpaper, a busy floral that twined about the room, sprawling, flamboyant. The vines and flowers sprouted off in every direction, and just the effort of tracing their progress along the wall made my head pound. And the clusters of pattern, just here and there, looked eerily like faces. No wonder people in this house had issues.

My stomach let me know it was closing in on noon, and the morning coffee and toast I'd swallowed before ferrying a surly D.J. to school again had been barely enough to get me through an hour. Unfortunately, the call of my stomach conflicted with my determination to avoid the jackals in the library. Intent on escape, I grabbed my purse and keys and headed downstairs. A cholesterol-laden lunch would do wonders for my mood.

"Know anyplace we can get a hoagie or a good cheesesteak around here?" I hadn't noticed Tony in my haste to get out the door. He stood by the entryway fireplace, examining the urn.

I wasn't feeling biddable. "Don't you have work to do?"

He got the hint. "Look, I know we kind of got off on the wrong foot last time," he said.

"You think?"

"And that—whatever that thing was with Sylvie..." He broke off, realizing that topic was off limits. "I understand you want nothing to do with this, Mary Catherine. And I don't blame you a bit. But everybody's got to eat, right?"

I took my time answering. "I suppose. Hoagies and cheesesteaks?" He nodded happily. "I used to know a place." In fact, I knew it well, though I hadn't sipped a Coke there in years. The corner coffee shop near the railroad bridge had always been packed Friday nights after football games. The hoagies were legendary.

* * *

After a brief detour to pat the ostracized Skippy, we took my car. Tony asked tedious questions about the area as we drove. How far to the train station? How much did a house go for around here? I parked in a municipal lot around the corner from the eatery, and together we crossed the street. The outside brick looked brighter, and green awnings covered the windows now. But the green and white tiled floor was the same, though the red banquettes had been replaced with café-style chairs and tables. Intent on ordering, we skirted them to perch at the counter.

Salads and biscotti and lattes had made inroads on the menu, but, thank God, the classics were still available. I went for the Italian hoagie, the roll baked fresh that day in the basement oven. Tony ordered a Philly cheesesteak and a side of onion rings. Obviously, neither of us had any social plans for later.

"So you grew up around here?" he asked, squirting ketchup onto the blanket of melted cheese and mound of golden rings.

"Just down the road. Eighteen long years." I didn't mind talking. Maybe the food had softened my resolve.

Tony bit into the sandwich and took his time chewing, his face reflecting something akin to bliss. "Can't have been all bad," he noted. The guy read subtext. Another surprise.

"It wasn't. Low crime. Good schools. Public transportation. Nearby culture and health care. Prompt snow removal." I knew I was being flippant, but just couldn't seem to stop myself.

He paused between bites to look at me. "So what was the problem?"

I sat straighter and swirled my straw. "Who says there was a problem?" I shrugged, defenses up.

"O-kay," he said cautiously. "You have any family left around here?"

This was a touchier point. "An aunt and some cousins in Montgomery County. We keep up through Christmas cards." I wiped my mouth with the napkin. "My parents are dead."

Tony raised his eyebrows at my phrasing. "Brothers and sisters?" He dug into the onion rings, giving them the attention they deserved. I took another bite of my hoagie, taking the time to swipe the dangling lettuce shreds into my mouth and chew before answering.

"Nope. Just me. How about you?" I glanced at his left hand. No ring.

"Lots of brothers and sisters. Giovanni, Joey, Angelica, Theresa, and Eileen."

I laughed when he said the last name. "What can I say, Mary Catherine Donavan? You're not the only one with an Irish grandmother." I noticed that his whole face lit up when

84

he smiled, and all of his wrinkles were laugh lines. I wanted to touch the dimple on his left cheek.

"My sisters are kinda scattered around the area now, but my two brothers are still in South Philly. So's my mom. She's almost eighty, but she cooks up a big Sunday dinner for the kids and grandkids every week." He slurped his water. "The old neighborhood's changed a lot. Ma says it's gotten too fancy for her, but she'll never leave."

Never leave. My mind wandered to Grey Crag and the fact that I was AWOL from my job. "We should be getting back. Mrs. Parrish might be wondering where I am."

"I think Peter's keeping her pretty occupied. He's really good at getting people to talk. All those years on the force." Tony took a twenty from his wallet without giving me a chance to see the check.

"Is that how you met him? On the police force?" I was having trouble imagining Tony in a uniform.

"Nah, he just needed somebody who knew how to operate a camera and do some editing. He asked around town, found me." He smiled again. "Sure beats wedding videos." He stood up, nearly upending a tiny table behind him. "Ready?"

We talked little on the ride back. I'd run out of pleasantries, and Tony was patting his stomach in appreciation of a decent meal. "Didn't know you could get something that good outside of the city," he commented. I wasn't about to try debating the merits of suburbs versus cities, so I turned on the radio and let the news channel fill the time until we turned up the long driveway.

"Thanks for the lunch," I said, my eyes focused straight ahead even after I turned off the ignition. "It's good to get out."

"Have to do it again sometime," he replied, wrestling briefly with the seatbelt and rolling out the door. He bent down and waited until I looked over. "See ya."

Inside, Mrs. Parrish was still enthralled by Peter's charm. Skippy had been sprung and tracked after Zina adoringly as she bustled about in search of dust and stray dog hair. I wandered to the back parlor and spent the next hour wondering if that had been a date.

* * *

It had become a routine of sorts — a quick cup of coffee before dropping D.J. off at school, sorting, organizing, and typing in the mornings, breaking for lunch, and more often than not, driving Tony to a local restaurant. Apparently, the Grey Crag investigation required a great deal of his technical expertise, considering the hours he spent on the premises. The rest of the crew must have been busy at some other location.

We fell into an uneasy friendship founded on proximity and food.

Day after day that September, Tony cheerfully sampled the diner's cheesecake, the deli's sandwiches, and the Italian place's cannolis. After the first week, I figured he'd appointed me his gustatory tour guide to the area. And I enjoyed the lunches, though they left a part of me that I didn't want to acknowledge still hungry.

As Tony worked his way through the menus, he told me about his brother's clashes in the South Philly business association, his sister's lousy husband, funny stories from his days as a videographer. Between bites, he entertained me with ridiculous accounts of the hoaxes his show had exposed. But he also listened, sitting absolutely still and devoting his full attention while I answered question after question. I told him a little about my career change and less about my home life. He didn't press, but once in a while, I caught him with a strange expression on his face while I was hedging about David or my childhood.

One day we'd gotten on the topic of nicknames and the power of calling a thing by its true name. "A rose just wouldn't be as sweet if we called it a stinkbud or a thornboggle," I insisted. "Or if Grey Crag were named Sunnyside or The Shambles."

"But a thing's the same no matter what you call it," Tony argued. "My grandmother calls me *Nonio*. It doesn't change who I am inside."

"But it speaks to your roots. And your relationships. It ties you to a past."

Tony remained unconvinced. "I'm still the same guy, no matter what my family calls me." The arrival of the steaming pizza distracted him for a moment. "It's not like I have one, all-powerful name that's, like, my essence or something."

"I hate my name," I confessed, spreading out a napkin. He waited for me to go on. "It's too much to live up to. The Virgin Mother. And the Catherine part's worse—martyred saint with a torture device named after her." I looked up from my half-eaten slice. "Did you know that Mary means 'bitter' in Hebrew?"

"Hmm." He still looked at me, ignoring his meal.

"I don't want to be like that."

"So don't," he said. As if was that simple. He took a sip of water. "What's your confirmation name?"

"God, I haven't thought of that in ages. Monica. Figures, doesn't it?" I stabbed my salad with vengeance and a fork. "Even the name I picked for myself ends up like a sick joke."

He regarded me steadily. "How's that?"

"The whole patron saint thing." I could feel the tears welling and willed myself to stop.

He took out his phone and entered the name, then read aloud. "Patron of wives and abuse victims." He glanced at me and then back at the screen. "Looks like once her husband died, she followed her son around for seventeen years trying to straighten him out." Seconds ticked away before he looked up at me again. "Maybe you could change your name to Bubbles."

When I laughed with him, I laughed at myself. It beat crying.

Chapter Thirteen

Bereaved women frequently report dreams in which the dead husband returns, like an incubus, and demands marital rights. While it is difficult to prove these cases, the vivid nature of the reports remains compelling.

The late October sun warmed the cavernous kitchen. Afternoon light spilled on the counters, splashed off the chrome stove, and puddled on the worn linoleum. There, spotlighted center stage, Skippy cowered next to Peter, whose blond crown bent in supplication. Both shrank before the barrage of Spanish and English launched from Zina, empress of the pantry.

"Cheese? You give that dog my cheese that I need for Mrs. P's dinner? You think cheese is good to feed to that *perro paludo*? He drops hair all over my house and you feed him my cheese?" Her arms windmilled, barely missing a bottle of balsamic vinegar.

The sardonic, self-possessed Peter hung his head lower. "I—"

Zina drew herself up to her full sixty-two inches and cornered him against the counter. Every word was a carving knife. "You got *nothing* you can say to me on this. What kind

89

of man are you, you treat your dog like that? Feed him cheese? Cheese is no meal for him. He needs meat. You get him good meat." She lifted her chin, daring him to argue.

Watching Peter reduced to sniveling was too precious to miss, so I stopped D.J. from passing through for his afternoon snack. Worked up, Zina lapsed into more Spanish, stroking the rough fur of Skippy's head as she spoke. Skippy's quivering expanded to a full-body wag. That betrayal was Peter's breaking point.

He knelt down—a considerable feat given his height— and scratched Skippy's ears. Gently, his hand clasped Zina's, and he looked up at her while she looked down on him. "You're right. I'll do better." And he smiled the smile of the angels.

"*Madre de Dios.*" Not even Zina the Warrior Princess was immune to that face. "You—you are a dangerous man."

The smile turned devilish. "I do my best." Peter drew himself to his full height. I gave her a standing ovation for not flinching. She held her righteous ground until Peter and his hairy *perro* skulked off, all three still smiling.

Recognizing the intermission for what it was, D.J. and I came in to root around for snacks. Of course, whenever food appeared, so did Tony. He surfaced as D.J. and I sat at the table going over assignments. By then, Zina had left, having finished Mrs. P's dinner despite the cheese crisis.

When the workday ended, I transitioned from companion back to mom, complete with a new set of hurdles. The scrawl on the notebook page before me represented the first. "They teach hieroglyphics now instead of cursive? What is this, kiddo?"

"Paper due tomorrow." D.J. bit into the apple I'd insisted he add to the chips he'd grabbed. "Hey, Tony."

Tony grinned. "Hi, kid. Oh, man. Corn chips." He plopped into the chair next to me so that I had to lean forward to see around him.

"What's the paper on?" I ignored Tony, whose leg accidentally bumped mine under the table.

"Proverbs. I have to pick one and explain why it is or isn't true." D.J. took another bite of apple. "It's so frigging stupid."

I looked over my glasses. "And you just got this assignment?" I already knew the answer.

"I can't think of a good proverb."

"How about 'Never put off until tomorrow what you can do today?'" My mom genes just can't be repressed.

Tony snorted, and D.J. rolled his eyes. "God, Mom. Like that's going to help."

I was just warming up. "Or 'Nothing ventured, nothing gained?'"

Tony reached for the chip bag, brushing his arm against mine. "Make hay while the sun shines."

I parried. "The way to a man's heart is through his stomach."

D.J. chimed in with a full mouth. "I think I need to research that one some more."

"And there's no time like the present," Tony added, digging into the bag.

D.J. stuffed the papers into his binder. "I got the idea now. You can stop."

Tony stretched across me to grab an apple from the bowl. I could see the muscles in his back pull beneath his rugby shirt. "What doesn't kill us makes us stronger."

It didn't seem as funny now. "I always hated that one," I said, pushing him aside. "It should be, 'That which doesn't kill us makes us miserable.'" I shoved my chair back and started gathering up the food.

Tony wiped his hands on his rumpled khakis, leaning back to look up at me. "Misery loves company," he said.

I knew my Shakespeare. "Misery acquaints a man with strange bedfellows."

Tony cleared his throat. "How about 'Strike while the iron is hot?'"

Somehow the duel had gotten beyond me and way beyond an essay assignment. "Once bitten, twice shy."

Tony rubbed the apple against his shirt. "Patience is a virtue."

D.J. looked from Tony to me and picked up his backpack. "Three's a crowd, guys. I'm going to my room." He headed up the back stairs.

Preoccupied, Tony tossed the apple from hand to hand. "Funny thing about apples."

Against my better judgment, I took the bait. "How's that? Other than they don't fall far from the tree?"

"They show up in so many myths." He admired the shining fruit in his hand. "So tempting." He held the apple towards me. "Want a bite?"

I did. I reached out and sunk my teeth in. The apple, tart and crisp, pooled its juice in my mouth. I chewed slowly to savor the tang. Watching every move, Tony waited. Oh, I knew this game. I licked my lips. He stood and stepped forward until we were only a whisper apart.

"How's it taste?" His voice was more of a growl. I leaned forward the extra inch to brush my lips against his. Then I bit.

"Ow!" His hand flew to his mouth.

"Once bitten," I explained.

His eyes smoldered with something hotter than anger. "You'll pay for that, Mrs. Livingston." He closed in, bumping the table. Behind me, the bowl of fruit clattered to the floor.

I sidled out of reach. "Thanks for sharing, Mr. Proforta." I grasped his wrist, rubbing my thumb across his palm. Then I dropped the apple in his hand and left the kitchen. I was still contemplating what would've happened if I'd taken the second bite when my cell rang. David. He started in before I'd even said a word.

"What the fuck is this I hear about some TV show, Mary Catherine?"

I immediately wished I hadn't picked up. "Way to start a conversation, David."

"D.J. just told me some shit about a haunted house and ghost hunters and how he's going to be famous."

I took a deep breath. "Well, it seems your son contacted that cable show *Paranormal Posse* and convinced them to come here. With my boss's approval. That's pretty much it." I wondered if I could get arrested for gagging a teenager.

"That's nuts!"

Patience is a virtue, I reminded myself. "I agree with you. But there's nothing I can do."

"This is what comes of your dragging him up there and filling his head with God knows what. You and you're damned self-actualizing."

I seethed and mentally transferred the gag to David. "This has nothing to do with my self-actualizing."

"I'm warning you, Mary Catherine. You took him with you because you said he needed a stable home environment. If things get more out of hand, I'm coming up there."

I spent the next five minutes pacing the hall with my phone, trying to downplay the whole fiasco. By the time I hung up, David was breathing evenly again, and I felt like I'd narrowly averted a disaster—David at Grey Crag. Such a bad idea.

CHAPTER FOURTEEN

I'd been right. David and Grey Crag were a bad combination. He showed up Tuesday morning, just as preparations for the taped investigation were underway, with a dry run scheduled for the day before the actual event.

All work on Mrs. Parrish's family history had been suspended. My companion duties had declined until all I did anymore was trail the woman around as she hung on every word from the pernicious Peter. For variety, I occasionally chased Skippy out and reminded my employer of social obligations that she then canceled. We were all sitting in the library — Mrs. Parrish, Peter, Tony, and I. The day was unseasonably warm, one of those edgy Indian summer days, and the stuffy room caused sweat to bloom under my tank top. Lazily, I scrawled notes as Peter explained, in tedious detail, the way the Scientific Overview of the Site would proceed. Any interruption was welcome. Well, almost.

Zina showed my meticulously groomed, supremely slick ex-husband in with undisguised glee, looking from him to me with twisted amusement. Skippy perked and scrambled to her side. Noting further evidence of Skippy's fickleness, Peter sulked. The rest of the room went so quiet, I could almost hear Mrs. Parrish's arthritic spine stiffen.

Shit.

"David. What are you doing here?" I hurried to the door, hoping to head him off. I wasn't quick enough.

"Came to check things out for myself." He glanced around. "Quite a place you got here."

Double shit.

"Um, let me introduce you to my employer, Mrs. Parrish. Mrs. Parrish, this is David Livingston, uh, D.J.'s father." After the initial shock, her genetically imprinted manners kicked in, and within a minute he'd thawed her with his megawatt grin. Then he moved on to impress the rest of the room.

Tony and Peter had risen by this point. David sized Peter up, and they looked like two Greek statues, perfect profile to perfect profile. If I hadn't wanted to hide under the sofa, I'd have taken a picture. David extended his hand first. "David Livingston."

"Peter Larsson." The contest escalated with David's handshake. Tony wisely hung in the background.

I stepped into the testosterone standoff before the alphas started arm wrestling. "Mrs. Parrish, do you mind if we take a break?"

"Oh, of course, dear, it's your husband. Of course you must go. I'll be quite all right here." She positively preened at the idea of having the posse to herself. I felt my cheeks redden. Where to take him? The small parlor was too close. If we went outside, they'd be able to see us from the windows. I pulled him towards the stairs while he held back, staring at the architecture. Zina smirked from the hall. Skippy wagged.

It took a lot of shoving, but eventually I maneuvered him into my room and shut the door, finally sure we couldn't be overheard. "What the hell, David?" I railed around to confront him, only to find he was much closer than I expected. I slammed flat into his unyielding chest. How could I have forgotten how big he was?

"I wanted to see what kind of place you brought our son to." I felt a twinge when he added, "I miss him, you know?"

"D.J.'s missed you too." I backed up, inner alarms sounding.

"Both of you." He pinioned me with that clear blue gaze, and I felt the old automatic response. "You look good, Mary Catherine. Thinner." He knew all my buttons and could press them or unbutton them at will. Momentarily, I lapsed as he slid his long-fingered hand up my bare arm, tracing the nerves along the sensitive skin. But I veered away before the hand slid further.

"So where are you staying?"

He glanced around the room. "Looks like you got plenty of room here." He cocked an eyebrow. "How's the bed?"

"Off limits. Get a hotel room."

"Stayed with you last time. We had some fun, as I remember. Bet D.J.'d love it if—"

"Don't try to get around me by using our son. I mean it." I backed up another step. "You found somebody else to warm your bed, remember? Three's too crowded for me."

"Looks like you've found some company of your own. You and that Larsson guy were sitting pretty close." He checked his reflection in the mirror over the dresser. His polo shirt exactly matched his eyes. He'd undoubtedly bought it for just that reason. "Just your type, isn't he?"

David had always had a problem with boundaries. I used to like that about him. "My private life's just that. Mine. And private." I opened the bedroom door. "You have to go." He needed more prodding. "I pick D.J. up at 2:30. Come back then."

* * *

After I managed to cajole him out of the room and through the front door, I tried to get back to work as if nothing had happened. Of course, that proved impossible. As soon as I walked into the library, I had to endure a trio of speculative stares. Tony's lasted the longest and unsettled me the most. For the rest of the morning, I refused to look at him. And I made sure I kept busy elsewhere throughout the afternoon, passing D.J. over to his dad when the time came and then hiding upstairs until I was sure the posse had ridden off into the sunset.

Assorted crew members traipsed in and out over the next few days, running wires, setting up motion detectors, testing ions in the air, and placing microphones. It got so that in every dark corner something flashed or beeped. D.J. dogged the technicians as soon as he came in the door, asking questions, touching sensitive instruments, and generally making a nuisance of himself. And David, who had business in Philadelphia, stubbornly stayed, which really threw me off. I was actually glad when he arrived to pick D.J. up and get him out from underfoot. My guilt level reached capacity when I saw the two so happy together, a matched set.

On strike because of the chaos, Zina had given up on shining any floorboards and kept to the kitchen with Skippy. Peter moped, finding myriad excuses to investigate the goings-on in the pantry region. Mrs. Parrish grew more twittery as her gracious home became a hive of activity. Long lunches with Tony were suspended. We had nothing to say to each other. For the time being, everything focused on the countdown. Dry run. Taping. Halloween. All Saints Day.

The Day of the Dead.

* * *

The kitchen was a disaster. Cardboard, crates, candles, potted marigolds, brown sugar, bananas and oranges, cigarettes, and an impressive lineup of liquor covered the counter from sink to refrigerator. The air was heavy with the scent of rising bread. And in the midst of the muddle stood D.J. and Zina, both bending over something. As I stepped in, I saw what it was. A skull.

"What the hell?" I had expected to find D.J. crouched over his homework, perhaps munching on cookies and milk.

"Hi, Mom. Isn't it cool?" D.J. was obviously delighted with the blue eyelashes that Zina was dotting on the skull with a pastry bag. "It's an *ofrenda*. Right?" He looked to Zina for confirmation.

"Everything on the whole altar is the *ofrenda, niño*. This is a *calavera*." She looked up at me. "The sugar skull. For *Dia de los Muertos*."

The Day of the Dead. My son was building an altar for the Day of the Dead. And he looked so happy about it.

"And we made dead bread too, Mom."

"*Pan de muerto*," Zina corrected. "So after we stack the cartons and cover the altar, we can start arranging things. You just need…" She nudged D.J.

"So, Mom, do you, um, have any family photo albums upstairs?"

I didn't like where this was going. Actually, I didn't like anything about this scenario. "I might. In the closet. Why?"

He chose the words carefully. "We need a picture. For the altar."

As I studied the lineup on the counter, I realized exactly who the offerings were for. I just couldn't understand why anyone would call her back. "You can go look. I'll stay here and talk with Zina." I waited until I couldn't hear his steps any longer.

"Just what do you think you're doing?"

Zina continued decorating the sugar skull with different colors of frosting. "D.J. is very troubled."

I crossed my arms. "I'm D.J.'s mother. If he's troubled, I'll deal with it."

She added frosting eyebrows in pink. "All this talk of death. It's not good for the young."

"It's not good for anyone. So why bring it into the kitchen?"

The line of frosting jiggled. "He wanted to build the altar. For his grandmother."

"I'm sure it wasn't his idea."

She finally put down the pastry bag. "You must feed the dead when they come to visit." She leaned over to turn on the oven. "It's not good to leave them hungry."

I forced myself to ask. "Why her?"

Zina turned and put a warm hand on my arm. Her eyes held mine. "You know why."

* * *

I hadn't leafed through the old leather photo album in years. The heavy black paper was tattered on the edges now. Some of the pictures had come loose from their cardboard points and slid into my lap when I turned the pages. The house I grew up in. Stella, the snippy family cat, staring balefully.

"Wow, who's this, Mom?" D.J. picked up a snapshot of a curvy coed straddling the bronze feet of young Ben Franklin on the University of Pennsylvania campus. She looked breezy and carefree and achingly young.

"What do you mean, who's that?" I snapped. I couldn't have changed that much, could I? So much that my own child wouldn't recognize me? "That's the girl your father fell in love with," I finally answered. "A lifetime ago."

I stuffed the loose photos haphazardly into the album and flipped to the front. "Here's what you're looking for." I took out a studio portrait taken when most women opted for tight perms or poodle cuts. My mother had kept her auburn hair long, always leaning more towards Lauren Bacall than Lucille Ball in appearance and temperament. She stared at the camera with the same defiance that Stella had cultivated.

"Wow," D.J repeated. The kid really needed to expand his vocabulary. "She looks like you, Mom." Out of the mouths of babes.

"Don't be ridiculous. We're absolutely nothing alike. Not at all." I pushed back from the table. "Make sure you put that album away where you found it. I don't want to see a trail of pictures all over the place." As a matter of fact, I didn't want to see those pictures at all.

* * *

The taping was only a day away. Staggering towards the stairs with an armload of Parrish photo albums from the forties and fifties, I caught sight of Tony and Peter. They were standing close together contemplating yet another pile of equipment and exchanging acronyms.

"The EVP monitor's portable, so that's no problem," Tony was saying. "Got to set up the EMF meter away from these cables and instruments though. Otherwise, it'll pick up interference. I was thinking of putting it in the hallway upstairs for the dry run tonight."

Peter nodded thoughtfully. "That would give us eyes on both floors at once. Any place special?"

"I need to take another look up there to make sure it's not near any registers or wiring." He called over to me. "Mary Catherine, okay if I follow you up?"

By that point, I was almost to the landing. "Knock yourself out," I said, and I meant it. But Tony took his time coming up behind me, and it was only when I reached the second floor and looked back that I got the distinct feeling he'd been watching my rear as I climbed. The tingle I felt had nothing to do with EVPs or EMFs or whatever other nonsense they were talking about. Looking ahead, I started down the hall, trying not to hurry.

"So your room's down this way?" Tony asked, keeping pace. He seemed to have forgotten about proper meter placement for the time being. I wasn't sure whether to feel annoyed or flattered, so I settled for uncomfortable.

"Down there," I answered, tilting my head. "I was just taking these up to catalogue in the quiet. The library's so noisy I can't think." The top album started to slip, and Tony reached out to grab it, nearly dropping the EMF meter. He tucked the machine firmly under one arm and took the rest of the pile from me in one smooth swoop.

"Where to?"

"Um, really, I had it. They're not heavy." He stood like a wall of bricks, waiting. "Uh, just down here." I led the way to my door and opened it. "I can take them now."

He ploughed by me into the room. "Where do you want them?"

"I guess just on the bed." My discomfort level rose even higher when he dumped the load in the middle of my mattress and sat on the edge.

"Jeez, who's your decorator? Lizzie Borden?" He looked around the room in wonder.

"It is kind of early-Victorian excess, isn't it?" I laughed. "I've gotten used to it. Feels almost like home now."

"Hate to see where you came from, then. How do you sleep at night?" He walked over to the wallpaper for a closer look. "It's like it's watching you."

"Thanks. I'll remember that when I turn off the light. Oh, look out!" Tony tripped over the box I'd left untouched, tipping it over. One flap worked its way loose and spilled a few of the contents on the floor. I hurried over at the same time Tony bent to help. We met in the middle.

"Sorry," he said, looking down at the objects he'd picked up. It took him a few seconds to process exactly what he held before he dropped the C-ring back in the box. I was just as quick to scoop up the fuzzy handcuffs. I kicked the leather bustier under the bed and stuck the bottle of massage oil in my back pocket.

"I haven't really gotten around to unpacking everything," I explained.

"Yeah, I know how that is. I still have boxes of textbooks from college."

"Right, you tend to unpack just what you need at first, and..." My voice faded out as I slowly shrank from embarrassment.

"Mary Catherine, may I ask you just one question?"

"No."

CHAPTER FIFTEEN

Another favorite trope of horror conventions is the Last Girl Standing, the requisite spunky female, unassailable and unflinching.

I thought about that encounter later that night as I locked my bedroom door, shed my tired clothes, and dragged my favorite nightgown off the peg. The rosebuds dotting the flannel were fading to pink, but the material was nicely broken in, and the missing buttons on the bodice didn't matter since I never buttoned up the neck. It was like wrapping myself in a hug. David had hated this gown and the robe that matched it.

Downstairs, Tony remained on duty monitoring his electronic babies for glitches before the big event. David had taken D.J. out to watch the Phillies take on the Braves, and D.J. would spend the night—a Friday—in the extra bed in David's hotel room downtown. After David assured me our son would be adequately fed, I'd reluctantly given in, hugging D.J. goodbye and watching father and son from the door.

They'd been heading out just as Tony came in, casually dressed in jeans and a sweater. The three of them stood in the

105

drive, David self-assured, Tony laid back and speculative. Between them D.J. hovered, chatting alternately about the game and ghosts.

I cringed when David started in. "Back again already, Proforta?"

Tony shouldered a tripod. "Well, you know, in this business, there's a lot of night work." His smile didn't reach his eyes.

David added up and drew the conclusion. He turned rigid. "You're staying the night?"

This time, Tony's smile was real. "Tonight's my best shot at getting what I need."

* * *

When I turned off the light and climbed up in that creaking bed, I tried not to think at all, but fragments of the day and evening surfaced unbidden. I thought about the wallpaper. I thought about Tony's expression when he realized what was in the box. I thought about the awkward supper we shared later in the kitchen, my back to that awful Technicolor altar. I thought about how much louder all the machines sounded after Mrs. Parrish floated off to her wing on the other side of the house. And I thought about Tony, now downstairs — alone.

The noises started after midnight somewhere in the hall outside, a tapping so soft I wasn't sure I heard it. Later came faint voices, as if a TV had been left on in one of the adjacent bedrooms. Old houses, I told myself. They croak and settle and breathe, forcing air through dusty vents to spread from basement to attic. The silences between the sounds were even more stressful as I lay in the dark straining to hear what might come next.

No, I was not going to go look to see what rattled my doorknob. I really was not going to open the door to confront whatever was making those soft pattering noises that reminded me of small, damp hands on the door panel, seeking a way in. And as the tapping turned to pounding and the pounding swelled until it felt like it was inside me, I was glad that D.J. was safe with David.

The pounding moved on to other doors and lower, to the stairway, then the landing. I traced it in my head through the entryway, past the fireplace and urn, through the archway, across the dining room and to the back parlor. I sat up. Tony.

Every horror movie I'd ever watched taught me to stay in my room with my charged cell phone and a decent weapon — a chainsaw, at the very least. What I should've done when I first heard the noise was take a swig out of the bottle in my dresser, pull the covers over my head, and ignore the rising sense of doom. That's what a reasonable woman would have done. But instead, like every horror movie cliché, I got up and grabbed my glasses.

At first, I cracked the door, peering left and right. A sconce burned at the far end of the hall, and I could see Penrod calmly licking his tail in the yellow light. Belting my robe, I crept out the door, past tables and mirrors, to the top of the steps. The carpet lay thick beneath my bare feet, muffling my footsteps so I moved like a ghost. Ahead, moonlight filtered grey through the stained glass. The stairs appeared empty.

Hugging the wall, I glanced back every few steps in case something came up behind me. There seemed to be more steps than I remembered. Disoriented, I stood suspended on the landing. Listening. Considering. It took a heart-ripping crash from below to send me racing down onto the parquet. Blood pounded in my ears as I searched frantically for the cause.

On the opposite wall, the fireplace glowered. The flicker rose and resolved into a ball of sick greenish light. Against every instinct, I edged towards it, foot by foot. Until I screamed.

"Mary Catherine!" Tony must've been close by, judging by the volume of his shout. "What? What happened?" He grabbed my arms and turned me around. "Are you hurt?" He spoke even louder now. "Holy shit, did you see that?" Tony stood wild-eyed beside me, breathing hard, clutching me to his heaving chest. Behind him, the red eye of the video camera winked.

"I stepped on something," I snapped, snatching my arm away and bending over to draw a ceramic sliver from my big toe. Beneath my bare feet, I felt a strange mix of powder and grit. The urn on the mantel lay shattered on the cold hearth. Yuck.

"You must've seen something." His incredulous expression tugged a little at my sympathy center, but only a little. Most of my sympathy was for my lacerated toe. I wondered when my last tetanus shot had been.

"Nope. Nothing." After years in the classroom, I could stonewall with the best of them.

"Come on. You must've seen it." Tony's pitch was several tones higher than usual.

"I didn't see anything." I worked to keep my voice calm and my hands still at my sides.

"You were right there." He paced to the dining room door and back in stabbing strides. Fortunately, the carpet was well made.

"I didn't see a thing." I stayed as still as possible, melting into the paneling as best I could.

He took off his glasses to rub his face as if the act could erase what he'd witnessed. "But you had to have seen something." He halted in front of me, accusing me with those chocolate eyes. As a protective measure, I lowered mine. He didn't back off, and the heat built between us.

Finally, I looked up, meeting the challenge. "Why?" He'd made a crack in my carefully protected façade, but that didn't mean I wouldn't defend the perimeter.

His forehead wrinkled, and his mouth hung open. "What?" I had him confused and off track. This was better.

"*Why* do I have to see something, Tony?" I fired back, meeting him glare for glare. I hadn't realized I was angry.

"What do you mean, *why*?"

"Just that. Why the hell do I *have* to see it?" The fire had roared up from nowhere, sweeping over me. I felt my face burn.

"That's a frigging crazy question." He dragged his fingers through his hair until the black curls stood up like horns. "You see it because it's there." He turned back towards the hall, searching for what he'd thought he'd seen.

"Did you *want* to see it?"

"What?" He turned back.

"You heard me." This time, I'd dug in for the firestorm.

"You ask it like I have a choice. How can you not see what's there?" His frustration level had reached the critical point, given the volume and resumed pacing, but I didn't even try to douse my temper.

"People choose not to see things all the time," I spit back. "Teachers don't see plagiarism. Wives don't see suspicious charges on the credit card. Fathers don't see bruises on their daughters." Though I tried to keep the flame blazing, tears welled and started to spill. For once, Tony seemed speechless. The pacing stopped an arm's length from me. If I'd been feeling stronger, I'd have called a time out to enjoy the quiet.

"So," he began carefully, "can you tell me what it is you choose not to see around here?"

"I need this job."

"I know, honey."

"I can do this job as long as I don't see things." I rubbed my nose on my sleeve.

"Like what things?" The gentle tone eroded the wall's outer layer, but it was the act of brushing my bangs from my eyes that sent it tumbling.

"Like—like the shadow man in the corner of the back parlor," I sniffed. "The one that watches me at night." Without breaking his gaze, Tony reached into his pocket and extracted a tissue. A guy who carries tissues. I hadn't thought such a creature existed.

"Do you see it anywhere else?" He pulled off my glasses, laid them on the mantel, and dabbed at my cheek. I could tell he was treading very carefully, like a cat picking its way along a buffet table.

"No," I hiccupped, "he stays there. It's kind of a relief, because at least I know he won't pop up just anywhere."

Tony leaned forward slowly, and, with his forefinger, tilted my chin until I met his eyes. "Does something else just 'pop up' on you?"

I had to smile a little at the totally inappropriate vision that came to mind before I banished it. "I also don't see Aunt Beatrice pulling her hairs out one by one to add to the giant nest in the bed at the end of my hall." He worked to keep his face impassive, but the eyes widened.

"And?"

"I really don't see the thing hanging from the upstairs railing. The thing that dangles just above the landing where the cat sits." I started to laugh. "I find it's easier not to see if I stay to the far right and keep my eyes on the carpet. Or don't wear my glasses." I took them from him.

"Impressive coping mechanisms." His gaze was starting to unnerve me.

"Lifetime of coping experience," I shrugged, looking down. "That which doesn't kill you, you know."

"Added bonus—without your glasses, I can see you better."

I sniffled some more. "You sound like the Big Bad Wolf."

He smiled and leaned closer. "You tagged me." The last clear thought I had was that he smelled like cookies.

The kiss started softly, just a graze of lips. But that spark I thought the tears had drowned spread, and I pressed back. He was more solid than I expected, muscles tensing as the kiss deepened. Then his hand started tracing those soothing circles on my back. Mortified, I broke away, pushing my hair out of my face and retying my robe. "Oh, God, you must think I'm so incredibly easy."

Tony put one hand out against the wall to steady himself while I fought the urge to go back into his arms. He looked at me, bemused, for a few seconds. Then his deep laugh rolled on and on while my humiliation spread. "Mary Catherine Donavan," he choked, draping an arm around my shoulders, "there's nothing that's easy about you."

It was only much later that I remembered the camera had been running.

CHAPTER SIXTEEN

Blood was oozing under my foot, impossible to ignore. Even worse was the mess on the hearth, and Zina wouldn't be back until Monday. Mrs. Parrish would have a heart attack if she had to sift through what remained of her dear departed, separating shards of bone from shards of urn. Mindful of my job description, I tried to put some iron back into my constitution.

I hobbled to the powder room to wrap my toe in tissue, having exhausted Tony's supply. Then I limped to the kitchen to collect Zina's stockpile of cleaning supplies. With a few swipes, I mopped the blood. At that point, Tony spurred himself to do something useful. I had him hold the dustpan while I swept up the cremains and emptied them into a Tupperware container, which I stowed in the pantry next to the shortbread. At least it was out of the way there.

Housework finished, I couldn't postpone the inevitable. "Tony, we'd better check out the rest of the house."

But he'd stopped listening. Now he was bent over his cell phone, his glasses, like mine, back in place. "I gotta warn Peter. This taping thing tomorrow—today—isn't looking good right now. I mean, the whole show's built on the 'there's no such thing as ghosts' shtick."

I tried again. "The bad news can wait an hour. We have to see if there's any other damage. Make sure Mrs. Parrish is okay." He still didn't put down the phone.

I walked over to him and punched his arm. "Tony, come on."

"Peter's never going to buy this." He finally looked up from the screen. "But you saw it, right? By the fireplace?" So he was back to that.

"Of course I saw it. So what? There's nothing in the dark that isn't here in the light."

He stood in the corner of the kitchen near the makeshift altar, staring at me for several seconds. "You are certifiable, you know that?"

I looked over his shoulder. Food and drink offerings, leaning heavily towards scotch and chocolate, spanned the lowest tier of the white-draped altar. On the top tier, yellow flowers, shrouded candles, and grinning sugar skulls covered every inch. Forcing myself, I confronted the picture propped on the center tier. The familiar auburn hair, arched brows, high cheekbones, narrow nose, blood-red lipstick, and unstinting gaze looked right back. "Yeah, well, I come by it naturally."

Enough was enough, I thought. "You share some responsibility here, you know. If you and Peter hadn't pushed your way in, none of this would've happened. So you can get your ass in gear and make sure nothing else has gone wrong. Or you can stay here with your phone and keep my mother company while I check on Mrs. P." For good measure, I added, "If I were you, I'd choose whatever's out there."

So we proceeded down hallways, turning on light after light. We snaked by the orb next to the chimneypiece and through the back parlor, where I ignored the thing in the corner. Then we climbed up the steps past an unconcerned Penrod, but steering wide of the feet hanging from above. Around the corner, we peeked into the bedroom where the blood still gleamed fresh years later. And on we went to the hairy nest at the end of the hall and back.

In the east wing, a bewildered Mrs. Parrish assured us she was fine and not to worry too much about the urn before stumbling back to her bed. So after an hour, only one room remained unchecked. My own.

Maybe the human body can take only so much before circuits overload. I shut my eyes to the leering wallpaper and shifting shadows and tuned out the faint taps. All I could think of at that point was the half-full bottle of whiskey in the dresser drawer.

Tony hovered in the doorway, so I waved him in. "Might as well join me. You need this as much as I do." I didn't care how he interpreted that statement.

* * *

The first shot was mine. And the second. Then I passed him the tea-stained mug and the liquor. "It's going to take more than a shot to make me forget this night," he muttered.

That stung. "So you want to forget everything about tonight."

He poured a second shot. "Hell, yes."

"*Every* part of the night?" Even that kiss? Had it mean nothing to him? Or was I just part of the general horror?

"Absolutely. The whole shebang," he said. I snatched the bottle away before he poured a third. "Hey, what gives?" He reached, and I backed up to the bed, holding the bottle behind me.

"Asshole."

Tony jerked his head as if I'd slapped him, which I had briefly considered, but I hadn't wanted to risk spilling the whiskey. "What got into you all of a sudden?"

That was the question, wasn't it? My laugh sounded maniacal. It wasn't the broken urn that toppled to the hearth by itself. It wasn't the full house of Crypt Keeper candidates. It wasn't the late hour. Maybe it was the spirits. I brought the bottle to my lips. "I'm suddenly feeling less generous." Since he still had the mug, I took a swig. "I think you'd better go. You'll have plenty of company out there." I nodded to the door.

Tony weighed his options. "But the booze is in here." He lunged. I evaded.

"No way. Go find your own. Maybe you can share a drink in the kitchen with my mother. There's quite a selection on that Day of the Dead altar." The bed creaked when he leaned in to get behind me. I feinted, but he was stronger than I gave him credit for.

The struggle had nothing to do with the whiskey. It had everything to do with the frustrating hours that led to this moment and left us wrestling on the bed. Eyeglasses flew. Whiskey splashed as Tony stretched to one side to set the hard-won bottle on the bedside table, pinning me between his arms. And there we hung in the balance.

"Maybe I don't want to forget *everything* about tonight," he ground out. "And to hell with patience."

"I—" The look he gave me shut me up. His dark eyes bored into me, and there was nothing tender there. Then, as if reaching some important decision, he bent his head and slowly licked the amber drops from my neck.

"Intoxicating," he murmured as he trailed his mouth up my jaw line, and that sensation, combined with the adrenaline and the fear and the anger, pushed me that much too far. The next kiss held nothing back. When he finally reached my mouth, his tongue delved deep while his hands cradled my head, angling for better penetration. I forgot to breathe. Without a conscious thought, I wrapped my arms around him and dug my fingers into his shoulders. It had been months…

* * *

The springs complained. And still I didn't turn away, not when he coaxed my mouth open again, not when he shifted to tug at my robe and cup my breast. And I said nothing when he ended the kiss to explore my neck further, thick stubble marking my skin as he slid his face down past my collar bone, over my breast, and still further, where the nipple peaked against the red flannel roses. It wasn't until he'd nosed aside the nightgown and started to feast on the flesh laid bare that I felt a stab of panic along with the sharp pull in my loins.

And I stamped on that panic, turned it to something darker. When I slid my hand around to the front and pushed his sweater up, I could feel his chest against my own. "More," I breathed.

"More," he agreed, reaching down to the hem of the nightgown. His palm was hot and impatient as it moved up my calf, past the ticklish skin on the back of my knee. And higher.

"God, I love your ass," he whispered. "It drives me up a fucking wall."

Now this was news. But I had no time to dwell on it because he'd started kneading said ass and pushing against me. The denim of his jeans scraped against the skin of my thighs and I spread them, wet and panting at the sensation, wanting all he could give. He nipped at my neck, unrelenting as he prodded between my legs. Our breathing turned labored. I reached to pull his hips even closer and start a rhythm to soothe the ache. "More."

He thrust against me, hard. It wasn't enough. Trying to release him, I slipped a hand between us, struggling with the buckle, the zipper. His laugh halted on a choke when I scraped my nails over his freed erection. It had been so long since I'd felt the press and need of a man. A long time since I'd wanted to. Suddenly, there was too much fabric separating us, too much pent-up demand.

With one hand he shoved down his boxers and jeans, using the other to nudge my thighs further apart, teasing the tender skin. I shivered. "More," he promised, spreading the swollen folds and rubbing insistent fingertips around the sensitive nub. I bucked, feeling the orgasm start and swell. It took hold and spread when he pushed his finger deep inside. He groaned and twisted, and my muscles tightened. The unbearable tension built. Peaked. And finally exploded.

He struggled to kick off his shoes and wrestle off the jeans. Took less time to strip me of my robe and nightgown. Then he froze above me, looking down. The breath stalled in my lungs. Exposed, I squirmed, horribly aware of every excess pound of flesh I'd kept hidden, every flaw now displayed. Where was that robe?

And still he stared.

Slowly, his caress glided from knee to thigh, over curve of hip to dip of waist and up again to the swell of my breast, settling over my still-pounding heart. "David's an idiot," he whispered, bending to take my nipple into his mouth, sucking hard. And with that, I was lost again.

I pulled him to me, straining, reaching down to where his erection lay hot and heavy against me, so thick my hand couldn't quite encompass it. So different. Intriguing. His breath hissed between his teeth. "More," I demanded, squeezing my hand down the smooth shaft.

He clenched his jaw and shifted. "You're sure it's all right? You're covered?"

"You cover me just fine. Now. Please." I couldn't think. I could do nothing but bring him closer.

He slid into me, stretching, pushing deep, bringing us face to face. Then he just held himself there, unmoving. I had an eternity to second guess the decision before he was thrusting steadily, his broad chest a deep red beneath the mass of black curls. Too late now. Abandoning thought and reserve, I took up the rhythm, matched him with all the bottled-up frustration of months, eyes open. The cords of his neck stood out. Every stout muscle in his frame grew taut as he bore down, eyes squeezed shut. I arched, closing around him. Another spiral spun out of control. Burst. Then the hot flood, the gut-twisting cry, and he collapsed on top of me.

* * *

Breathing was overrated, I decided as I lay buried beneath him, waiting for my heart to slow down. I contented myself with stroking his back, now slick with sweat. I could breathe later. Much later, I thought, pelvis still throbbing. But the need for oxygen had me poking him in the ribs.

"No more," he mumbled.

I poked again. "Tony, I can't breathe."

He shifted so that my lungs could expand enough to fuel a giggle.

His brows contracted. "What now?"

Above me, he looked like a cherub, cheeks rosy, wild curls framing his face, lips pouting and full. But his eyes were half-lidded in the aftermath of sex, and no cherub sported such a thick beard. I figured it was best to keep my thoughts to myself. "I was just thinking about your question. About what got into me. Looks like you did."

He scraped his beard against my breast, making me giggle again. "You are one exasperating female, Mary, my girl." Rolling over on his back, he folded me under his arm, my head tucked into his neck. He kissed my forehead and drew up the covers.

My girl. I poked at that too, examining the phrase from every side while I twined my fingers through his springy chest hair.

"You said it's safe, right?' he rumbled sleepily.

"We checked every room." I snuggled closer. I couldn't remember the last time I'd felt this good.

"I mean you're protected, right? On the pill?"

I stopped twirling patterns on his chest.

Chapter Seventeen

Subversion of the Last Girl Standing trope came after the initial spate of slashers. This later incarnation of the "final girl" gets to have sex and still kill the monsters.

"Mary Catherine?" I felt him stiffen under my hand, but this time, it wasn't in the good way. He rolled to his side to face me. "Christ, you're not going to tell me that you let me —"

I scrambled across the bed, desperately searching for my robe. Shit. Oh shit.

"Give me a break, Tony, I wasn't planning —"

"For God's sake, woman, how old are you? Sixteen?" He pushed off the bed to find his jeans. "Don't you know that this is the age of AIDS? Herpes?"

"You — you have a venereal disease?"

"What? No, of course I don't — but — oh, fuck, Mary Catherine. Don't change the subject." He grabbed me by both arms, jeans around his knees. "Did you ever consider that I might get you pregnant?"

Time stopped. "No," I stated baldly, clutching the robe to my chest. "I didn't. David — David had a vasectomy. Right

121

after D.J. So—no." I wondered if I could just crawl under the bed and die there.

His hold loosened. "So other than your husband..." he said slowly.

"Ex-husband." I wanted that clear.

"Oh, fuck." Tony pulled up the jeans and bent down to collect his shirt, boxers, and shoes. I noticed he'd never bothered to take off the black socks. "Damn it, Mary Catherine, I knew you'd be nothing but trouble." He shook his head, trying to clear it. "Look, we're both tired, and I've got a long day ahead of me. We'll talk later."

Around the edge of the drapes, I could see the first hint of dawn. "No, we won't. Because I'm going down to make coffee. I plan to drink the full pot. Then I'm going to take a very long shower and forget I ever met you, Anthony Proforta." And I stalked out of the room.

* * *

Scalding coffee and a boiling shower brought me to my senses. I swore at myself as I scrubbed the whisker burns on my chest, cursing my stupidity. While I pulled on underwear, cargo pants, and an old sweatshirt, I cursed Tony and the van he rode in on. I shoved my feet into sneakers and pulled my damp hair back into a scrunchy, imagining it twisted around his fat neck. A careful look at the calendar reassured me that my mistake with Tony wouldn't turn into a mistake nine months down the road. Finally calmer, I was collecting my keys and purse from the back parlor when I heard the tap on the door.

"I see you have your protective armor back in place," Tony said, leaning against the door jamb.

"Excuse me?" The tone should have frozen him solid through the next Ice Age.

Unscathed, he stepped closer, slipping his hand under the baggy sweatshirt. "You dress like a teenage boy." The hand roamed. I fixed him with an icy glare and leaned back.

"What I choose to wear shouldn't affect you in the least, Mr. Proforta."

"You're right, Mrs. Livingston. It's not nearly as interesting as what's under it. Though I find myself surprisingly attracted to red flannel rosebuds." He started to nuzzle my neck. Before he found a chink in my armor, I pushed him away. Slinging my purse over my shoulder like a shield, I stalked into the hallway, determined to make a dignified retreat.

But I had to weave my way around clumps of techies and their toys. It was the Saturday before Halloween, the day of the big taping. The Paranormal Posse was back in the saddle, ready to ride into action that night for the entertainment of nearly a million viewers. And in the middle of the bedlam, just behind Peter and Annoying Ashley, lounged David and D.J.

"Oh, here she is," David said smoothly, leaning down to kiss my cheek before I had time for an evasive maneuver. "As you can see, I brought our son back in one piece." On the periphery, I saw Tony join the throng, looking more than a little disreputable in broad daylight. David, as always, was impeccably groomed. You could slice an apple on the knife edge of his pressed slacks.

David raised his eyebrows at the bright smile and cheery tone I summoned. "Thanks for driving him back. Hope you both had a good time." He really did have dreamy blue eyes, I thought. And his own talents. And he was trying to make amends. I widened the smile a fraction.

David looked from me to Tony, who now stood a few feet away, arms crossed, scowling. Then he returned my smile, tinged with a touch of triumph. "Yeah. It was great. Went down to the bottom of the ninth. Rollins hit a home run. How about you?" Tony quickly muffled his laugh, and David's eyes narrowed.

"My night was deadly dull," I assured him. "I'd give anything to escape for a decent evening out—one as far away from this craziness as I can get." I made sure to look directly at Tony, who reddened just a tad.

David had his faults, but he never passed up a promising opportunity. "It just so happens that there's a French restaurant not too far from my hotel that has an excellent wine list." His hand moved to my waist.

"Well, we do need to iron out some things about D.J.'s health insurance. And I like—

His thumb rubbed against my rib. "I know what you like. Seven?"

Since D.J. had already arranged to watch the evening's excitement from off camera, I was free to get the hell out of Dodge. "Seven it is." I ignored my better angel, who was screaming in my right ear at that point. I knew better, since I had a long history of bad decisions involving this man. I just didn't care.

When I walked out the door, I didn't even consider pulling down the sweatshirt over my backside, just in case anyone was watching.

In half an hour, I reached the big mall, where Nordstrom's, Neiman Marcus, and Lord and Taylor beckoned. My paycheck was burning a hole through my wallet, and my purse was ready to burst into flames at any moment, just like my temper. Adolescent boy, my ass, I thought as I left the lingerie department with a red lace demi bra, garter, and sheer black stockings.

Searching rack after rack, I found a sultry dress in crimson, its asymmetrical neck plunging enough to show off my assets, its princess seams sweeping to a V in back. Beneath, the Spandex underskirt molded my hips, and a high back vent made it possible to walk in the pencil skirt. Of course, walking would be a challenge in the teetering heels I added to the purchases. A final stop at the makeup counter and I was back on the road to Grey Crag. After force-feeding D.J. a healthy lunch, I sneaked up the back stairs to avoid the commotion below. I dumped my spoils on the rumpled bedspread that still smelled faintly of sex and got to work on my gender transformation.

After shaving every body part I could reach, I slathered my skin with lotion. Painstakingly, I worked the flat iron through each strand of hair on my head until the mane gleamed like polished mahogany. Leaning close to the vanity mirror, I applied the new foundation, blush, liner, mascara, and a lipstick that left bloody kisses on the tissue when I blotted my lips. I sprayed the scent David gave me last Christmas on my neck and on the back of my knee. Finally, I strapped myself into the bra and garter, inched the sheer stockings up my newly smooth legs, and stepped into the towering heels.

Although I didn't recognize the reflection in the mirror, she sure didn't look like a boy.

Taping was scheduled to begin at eight, so floodlights illuminated the grand staircase when I descended, using the banister instead of hugging the wall. With grit, I could pull off a Scarlett O'Hara impersonation, I told myself. At least the Carol Burnett version.

"You look nice, Mom," D.J. said as I passed him on the landing. But nice wasn't what I was aiming for. "Well, if it isn't the lady in red," Peter called from across the floor, assessing as he nudged Tony. That was marginally better. But the rat bastard Tony didn't say a word, even when I made a point of walking past him so he could see how far that push-up bra could push. I took great pleasure in the fact that in my new heels, I was taller than he was by an inch.

"That's one hell of a dress, M.C.," David said, holding out his arm. Well, at least someone was paying attention, even if it was the wrong someone. I glanced over, but Tony had nothing to add. He did look like something had gone down the wrong way, however. I was shallow enough to hope he choked.

"Thanks, David. Shall we?"

He bowed close. "I was hoping we would," he whispered. "That outfit's an invitation all by itself, you know."

I felt a twinge and gave him my quelling look. "Dinner and conversation, David," I murmured. "That's all the invitation covers." But David remained attentive, holding the door of his rental sedan for me while I slithered in, determined not to think about the performance at Grey Crag for the rest of the night.

Later, he held my seat at the Center City restaurant. Throughout the meal, I kept wondering who this charming stranger was and what he'd done with my ex-husband. But the new guy was pleasant, especially in the wake of Terrible Tony. And the poached Asian pears, Ahi tuna, and crème brulée were a far cry from an Italian hoagie.

We'd finished the bottle of Pinot Gris from Alsace that David selected, and I was wondering if I'd ever be able to peel myself out of that dress when he offered to help. I should've seen it coming.

"You know, Mary Catherine, my room's right upstairs. With a nice view of the fountain."

"I bet D.J. loved it."

David laughed, sliding his arm along the top of my chair. "He liked the flat screen TV." He lowered his voice and his hand. "You look especially delicious tonight."

"David, you already ate your dessert. Wasn't the chocolate soufflé enough?" Stupid comment. It gave him an opening.

"Now that you mention it, no." He leaned closer, though the tables were far enough apart that no one could overhear. "Seeing you like this," he looked down my bodice, "brings back memories." He kissed my temple. "Remember how we used to play?"

Well, I did. And I had a box full of toys still sitting under my bed in case I forgot. Towards the end of our marriage, it took every toy in the toy chest to get David motivated. I'd worried about carpel tunnel syndrome until he found another playmate. "I do, David. But you decided to play with Alexa. And I never was good at sharing my toys." I hitched my chair further away. "Only child syndrome."

"Alexa won't play as nice as you."

So that was it—the little vixen wasn't kinky enough for the long haul. I felt like a tart. "That's too bad. I'd heard she had such youth and…stamina."

He at least had the grace to look uncomfortable. "I was mad when I said that."

I toyed with the wine glass. "That makes two of us."

He laid his hand over mine. "Let me make it up to you." He leaned in for the kill. "I did buy you dinner."

I reclaimed my hand and dropped the linen napkin on the table. Though it would be so easy to fall into our old patterns, I was following a new playbook now—with all the men I had the misfortune to know. "Sorry, David, but I'm not on the dessert menu tonight."

127

"So I just keep on paying, is that it?" The waiter looked up from across the room.

"Hush. People can hear you. Anyway, we should be getting back to check on D.J. He gets carried away with this Paranormal Posse crap."

He frowned as he took out his credit card. "You never used to be like this." I took that as a compliment.

* * *

It was past midnight when David parked in the drive and walked me to the door. Though most of the posse vehicles seemed to have left the corral, the van was still out front. So was Penrod, tail twitching.

"Do I get a goodnight kiss, at least? For old times' sake?" He was already bending down. Under the circumstances, it seemed rude to refuse. And it was all so familiar, the taste, the feel of him in my arms. The breeze as he reached up my skirt. The yowl.

"What the hell was that?" David's head shot up, but Penrod had already streaked behind the bushes.

"Just the cat." David looked ready to launch into his *felines are the spawn of Satan* spiel, so I quickly added, "Thanks again for dinner."

His temper flared. I was reminded of D.J. at two when I put him in time out. "So you're still not inviting me in?" I shook my head regretfully. He blustered. I smiled, patted his cheek, and closed the door behind me. Finally spent, I leaned against it. It was a few minutes before I heard him drive away, spitting gravel. I felt oddly like crying.

"Little late, aren't you?" Tony came out of the shadow by the steps.

"What are you, the house mother?"

"I thought that was *your* job, Mrs. Livingston. By the way, I sent your boy up to his room."

He stood between me and the stairs, but I was no coward now. I walked straight towards him. "Good. Hope he stayed out of your way. Wouldn't want him to interfere with all your important myth busting."

"As a matter of fact, everything was absolutely quiet tonight—just like the show predicts. Like clockwork. Another Paranormal Posse triumph." He paused. "But the recording from last night, well, that's another story."

I felt the air prickle as I slid by him and his leer. Since any answer would prolong a conversation I didn't want to have, I started up the stairs. Maybe I wasn't all that steady, given the wine, the turmoil, and the shoes, but I thought I managed pretty well.

"Careful. You're going to break your neck in those things." Tony was right behind me when I turned around. I wobbled, then caught myself and straightened to my full height plus heels.

"I'm perfectly fine, Mr. Proforta."

His chuckle just pissed me off. "Yeah, I can see that, Mary Catherine. Maybe you should take those things off before you try the rest of the stairs, though."

Much as I hated to agree with a word the aggravating man said, my feet hurt, and it was a long way up. When I hiked my dress so I could sit on the landing, I at least had the satisfaction of finally making him look. So I took my time slipping out of the shoes. For good measure, I unhooked the stockings from the garters and rolled them slowly down my legs. It did feel better. "Mind helping with the zipper? It's kind of hard to reach." I stood and turned my back to him.

When he eased the zipper down past my waist, I could feel the cold air at the base of my spine. But that was all I felt. He didn't say a thing. So as I turned back around, I made sure the dress gapped enough to show off the girlie new bra.

"Thanks, Tony. Pleasant dreams." And I bent over, picked up my shoes and stockings, and went to bed, not even sparing a glance for the bulging eyes and purple face of the woman hanging from the railing.

I slept like the dead.

CHAPTER EIGHTEEN

Dead. Oh God, I wished I were dead. Dead would've been kinder. My head had swollen to twice its size, and ground glass lined my eyelids. My mouth was so dry it felt like Bedouins could have set up camp in it. And the bed kept bouncing.

"Mom. Mom. You've got to see this."

I pulled the pillow over my head. "No, I don't. Go away. Eat something."

The bouncing stopped. "Just open one eye and look."

To stave off more bouncing, I peeked out from beneath the pillow. D.J.'s laptop hovered two inches from my face. He had YouTube up and running, and the blurry image on the screen looked suspiciously like Grey Crag. I blinked. "What the hell is this, D.J.?"

I should have been prepared for the renewed bounce. "It already has 34,623 hits! And it's only been up, like, fifteen hours!"

Once I untwisted my covers, I managed a sitting position. With D.J.'s help, I located my glasses, which he found inside the whiskey-stained mug. I silently prayed there was nothing else besides a ghost on that video. The computer screen came into focus. For the full minute and thirty-eight seconds, I sat transfixed by the video, watching the urn inch its way along the mantel and crash to the ground. The greenish glow I'd seen two nights before looked more like a floating ball on screen.

Peering over my glasses, I gave my son my full attention. "D.J., where did this come from?"

He didn't even have the sense to lie. "Well, Tony had this thing on his phone, right? And he was showing me and Peter and Mrs. Parrish, right? So I had my phone and…"

My head swelled further. "You copied this video from his phone and posted it on YouTube?"

"Wow, 34,701!"

I made a mental note to have the doctor check for ADD at the next checkup. "And did you have Tony's permission to copy his video and post it?" I took the silence for an answer. My churning gut already suspected the truth anyway. "You are in deep trouble, David John Livingston IV." The pending lawsuit loomed large. "Is the posse around?"

"Tony said they were going back to Posse Headquarters to analyze data. And they have to get ready for the next case."

I pulled myself into full mother mode. "Okay, kid, listen up. You are to remove this video immediately. Then you are going downstairs to make coffee. You will fill the biggest clean mug you can find and bring it to me. Now move." I staggered to the bathroom, avoiding the mirror when I brushed my teeth. The hot water didn't do much for my head, but at least I no longer felt like a dried-out sponge. By the time I was dressed in sweats, D.J. delivered the coffee. I drank it straight as I headed for the library to locate Peter's number. D.J., finally realizing the deep poop he'd dug into, followed.

I've had more uncomfortable moments. Childbirth, for instance. But at least the phone call to Posse HQ was short.

The actual yelling, cursing, and threatening lasted only halfway through the mug, and I manned up and listened to it all, holding the receiver so D.J. could share in the abuse. By the time I reached the bitter grounds, Peter had moved on to damage control. He said he'd be in touch. I had no doubt that was true.

David's reaction pretty much mirrored Peter's, though from David I heard more about my failure as a parent and what an unsuitable environment a twenty-room mansion on the Main Line was. I imagined a little David doll studded with pin after pin until he wound down. Thankfully, he was scheduled to fly back to Raleigh later that day, so at least I'd be spared a prolonged tirade in person. I passed off the phone so he could grill D.J. before contacting a lawyer.

Who ever said Sunday was a day of rest?

Mrs. Parrish, at least, seemed unconcerned about this newest invasion of her privacy. We shared a late breakfast in the kitchen—toast for me, herbed egg white omelet for her—while she filled me in on the taping the night before. "It was like the old days, Mrs. Livingston, back when Mr. Parrish was still alive. I so wish you had been here. People all over. Bright lights. Such excitement." She looked coy, and my stomach turned. "That nice Mr. Larsson says the show will air soon. I've already told all my friends. And the family's delighted."

I just didn't know what to say to that, so I said nothing.

CHAPTER NINETEEN

Whether we call it a prediction, an omen, an augur, or a coincidence, this occult phenomenon has been found in the historical record as long ago as the ancient Greeks and Romans.

I should have known that the day wasn't going to get any better. When I smeared jam on my morning toast, I accidentally crossed knives with Mrs. Parrish. A single crow squatted on the lawn when I ran to my car to get my phone charger. And when I came back in the kitchen, the broom I had been using to sweep the crumbs fell over. At that point, my grandmother would have been rushing to mass to light candles.

The Fates had control. They were turning cartwheels when Mrs. Parrish and I settled in the library, too restless to relax. After the evening's ruckus, she should have been worn out, but she seemed to hold a charge better than my cell phone. She picked through an album, growing a little teary at the pictures of men in uniform who never came back from St. Vith, Bastogne, and Hürtgen Forest. The energy seeped out of her as she turned the pages. In the sunlight, she looked her age and then some. So did I.

Out front, the sputter of an engine let us know we had a visitor. "Damn," I muttered from the bay window when I saw the van. "Please let it be Peter." I'd survive another of his assaults. But the full brunt of Tony's fury was something I didn't think I could weather. My stomach rebelled again when the engine died and the van door rolled open.

On the stone ledge below me, Penrod perched, tail lashing. Since the omens predicted the worst possible future, I really wasn't surprised when Skippy growled and sprang before Tony (yes, it had to be Tony, dressed for business) secured the leash. The cat took off with the dog in close pursuit.

I took my time getting to the front door. "Morning, Tony." That's about as much as I ventured after I got a good look at his clenched jaw.

"Nothing but trouble," he snarled, rivaling Skippy in menace.

I couldn't argue with that. "You coming in or…" I looked to my left, where Skippy bounded through the high grass on the hillside.

It really was kind of interesting to watch Tony's temper ebb and swell. The square jaw clamped tightly enough to crack a molar. Those full lips thinned to a grim line. His neck and shoulder muscles tensed under the white shirt. I tried to maintain a clinical detachment while the waves inside him raged, crashed, and slowly subsided, muscle by muscle, until he stemmed the red tide. By the time he answered, his temper and voice had calmed. "I need to go after him. Peter'll have my balls if anything happens to his damned dog." He loosened his tie and started back down the steps, then turned to look at me, thick eyebrows raised. "Coming?"

I hesitated since my sense of self-preservation remained strong. "Wasn't thinking of it."

"I could use some help here." He took a step closer. "And besides, you owe me."

I couldn't argue with that either. Sighing, I slammed the door behind me and followed him into the high grass. Grass is a fairly broad term for what grew in the acres beyond the trimmed lawn. Red-brown sedge, white snakeroot, purple asters, creamy milkweed, and goldenrod hid briars and bittersweet that snaked around my ankles and snagged fine, bloody trails across my skin. Every time I paused to untangle another snare, I fell farther behind. There was a metaphor in there somewhere, but my head hurt too much to dwell on it.

So what if Tony was keeping his distance? I couldn't really blame him, could I? He'd seen me at my naked, vulnerable worst. And obviously my best the night before hadn't been enough to erase that image. Besides, now that D.J. had stolen his video and ruined the entire Paranormal Posse premise, all that Tony wanted was to rip me limb from limb. He only asked me along because he needed help with Skippy. Or maybe he wanted to lure me into the open to do away with me once and for all.

By the time I'd extricated my foot from a groundhog hole, I wished he had put me out of my misery. We had crossed the span of Grey Crag's fiefdom, and ahead in the valley lay the winding road and bridge beneath the birches. The Fates did double flips. So did my miserable stomach.

Tony lounged outside the stone wall surrounding the sleeping graveyard. Beyond him, Skippy lifted a leg near a boxwood. If I'd eaten anything besides toast and jam, I'd have lost it at that moment, but the recent hike had burned up any residual calories.

"Come *on*, Mary Catherine. Hurry it up before he decides to take off again." Tony slipped through the gate, leaving me battling with myself by the wall. The brown and grey fieldstones were mortared in securely, so my kick hurt only my toe, still sore from its close encounter with the broken urn.

Fate. I had no choice. I scuffed up the white gravel path, through the gate, and into the shaded cemetery.

Ignoring us both, Skippy trotted past a bush and row of markers, sniffed an American flag, squeezed between two shriveling rosebushes, and stopped to smell a promising pile of leaves.

From the right, Tony edged towards him, hand outstretched. "Here, boy. Good dog. Come here, Skippy. Come here, you brainless fur bag."

Skippy paused in his sniffing to look at Tony and then at me, approaching stealthily to his left. He cocked his head to one side as I advanced, oh so slowly, closing the space between us. "What a nice puppy," I crooned. "What a good Skippy baby."

Maybe it was my insincere tone. Or maybe those Fates were bored with the show. But Skippy bolted, swerving around me and loping down the path.

"Fuck. Fuck. Fuck." Tony clomped towards me. "Why didn't you grab him when he ran by?"

I would have shouted back, but I was hyperventilating. "Right. You expect me to grab the Hound of the Baskervilles and wrestle him to the ground." Given the leash in his hand, I felt some concern for my safety.

"He went down that way. Maybe we can trap him between those buildings." Tony loped after Skippy. I was surprised he could generate that kind of speed, but it *was* downhill. He'd gone fifty yards before he realized I wasn't trotting behind him. "Are you coming?" he called, impatient.

"No."

"Come on, Mary Catherine."

I shook my head. "I'm done."

"I need you, damn it."

"I need to go." But I remained rooted on the path. He started back up the hill.

"What the fuck is wrong with you?"

"Stop swearing. This is a churchyard. God will smite you." I crossed my arms.

He marched back until he was right in front of me. "God'll be more pissed when I wring your neck. Maybe. Let's go."

I tugged away when he grabbed my arm. "I can't, Tony."

He threw the leash to the ground. "Why the hell not?"

"There's something down there."

"No shit."

"Something besides Skippy."

He finally got it. "Ah, no. Here too?" Tony sank to a nearby stump which, judging by its width, dated from the last century. He shook his head. "Nothing but trouble."

I finally felt something besides fear. "It's not my fault you can't control your dog." I headed for the gate, but he was too quick.

"I'll make this really simple, Mary Catherine. You are not leaving the graveyard until we have Skippy. I don't care if every spook from Dickens' *Christmas Carol* shows up."

That hit a nerve. My mother had been watching the Mr. Magoo version the night I left her alone. It was for only three hours because of the junior high Christmas Concert. Failure to show up meant a "D" in Chorus, and I'd been a grade grubber even then. She'd been into the scotch since Daddy missed the 4:30 train out of New York, and there was no way she could drive me, even if I'd wanted her to come. She hadn't been alone at night in years. We always made sure of that, because she saw things in the dark. But this once, this single, solitary time, I refused to give in and stay home with her.

She was often difficult around the holidays, had been worse than usual ever since the summer, and had sunk even lower that moonless night during the darkest time of year. She hated the dark, hated being alone with the voices and shadows. Rebellious and selfish, I didn't spare her more than a passing thought while I perspired under the hot stage lights, floated through the carols and applause, or shivered during the cold walk home. I didn't let myself think at all until I opened the front door. But those three hours apart had been enough.

We never did get the bloodstains out of the carpet. And I was still dealing with the other issues.

* * *

"Mary Catherine?" Judging by the look on Tony's face, I must have spaced out for a bit. "Come on, honey. I'll be right there with you. We just have to go down the hill, corner the dog, and then I'll take you to the diner and buy you some cheesecake."

I knew that man was evil the first moment I set eyes on him. It wasn't the cheesecake that tipped the balance, however. The Fates still had the upper hand. Miraculously, I was finally fed up with my cringing self. I'd manned up to Peter. I'd denied David. I could do this. Especially if there was cheesecake involved. "You're on. But there better be cherries on top."

* * *

The mausoleums had accumulated even more lichen and moss over the intervening years. While Skippy watered an abandoned pile of funeral wreaths, we closed in. This time Tony darted and I dodged. Tony's leather loafers skidded on the damp leaves, alerting Skippy. The ensuring tussle was hairy. I skinned a knee while snatching at the collar. Tony earned a bruise or two and muddied his khakis when he grabbed the beast around the middle, but Skippy twisted and squirmed away, enjoying the new game. He let out a deep-throated bark and hunched, happily panting between two tombs. With a heroic leap, Tony finally cornered the dog against a mossy wall. Skippy was tethered in minutes.

That wasn't so bad after all, I thought to myself. Next to me, the rough stone of the tomb sweated. I kept my nerves in check, even forcing myself to stroll over to the barred window. *See? Nothing to it*, I chided myself. I hoisted myself up to look inside.

Then the dark closed in like the lid of a coffin.

CHAPTER TWENTY

Hmmm. *At least somebody sprang for the deluxe coffin*, I thought when I felt the cushion underneath me. I could smell incense. Cautiously, I opened my eyes, praying I'd gone up instead of down. The barrel-vaulted ceiling reminded me of a tunnel. Perhaps loved ones waited on the other side. I bet it had been a lovely funeral. I wondered who'd done the eulogy. I hoped it hadn't been David.

"She's awake." I didn't think that was the voice of God. It sounded too much like Tony. No way Tony made it to heaven. I turned my head.

The last time Tony had hovered above me, we'd both been naked. "You have little gold flecks in your eyes," I observed. I enjoyed the confusion on his face.

"Do you think you can sit up now?" His concern was even better. I wondered how long I could milk it.

"You sure you don't want me to call for an ambulance?" A nervous man in a brown cardigan peered over Tony's shoulder. "She looks pretty pale."

"Late night last night," Tony shrugged, implying all sorts of sin to get the man to back off. It worked.

"Well, if you're sure. I'll be in the vestry. You let me know if you change your mind."

Tony glared a warning at me as he answered. "Thanks for your help, but we're fine now."

I sat up in the pew and looked around. Fine, my ass. "Bet they used this place as a hospital at one time."

The cardigan guy looked surprised. "Why, yes, it did serve as a temporary hospital. During the Revolutionary War. I can get you the brochure if you're interested, ma'am."

I nodded as I gazed at the stone floor and stark wooden pews. "Lots of them died in here." The cardigan guy backed farther away.

Tony narrowed his eyes. "Cut that out. You're scaring him."

I had the grace to feel a twinge of guilt. "Where's Skippy?" My sacrifice had better not have been in vain. My knee was starting to throb.

"I tied him to a post outside. By now, he's probably chewed through the leash." Tony sighed. "Do you think you can walk? Because if I have to carry you all the way back—"

"You carried me in here? By yourself?" I was oddly pleased.

He looked offended. "Just because I'm not some six-foot powerlifter doesn't mean I'm a pussy."

Mmmm. I was suddenly reminded of a Roman statue I'd seen in a Raleigh museum. The marble Hercules had been bulky, stocky and short—sort of like the thick club he carried. He was thick everywhere, another aspect that reminded me of Tony. Maybe carrying me was the equivalent of a thirteenth labor, certainly no tougher than bearing the weight of the world in exchange for the golden apples of the Hesperides. "Are you mad at me?" I smiled dreamily.

"Furious." He smiled back.

"Do I still get the cheesecake?"

"Let's start with getting you back to the house."

* * *

We took the route along the road this time, which, though longer, offered no obstacles and fewer distractions for Skippy, who trotted from one interesting smell to the next. Relaxing, Tony wrapped an arm around me, and I let him. Maybe he was making sure I didn't take another tumble, but I put that thought on hold for now and enjoyed the sensation of being tucked firmly into his side.

"You've really screwed up my day, Mary Catherine. And my job. You know that?"

He didn't sound angry, so I didn't get my back up. "I'm good at screwing," I quipped, perversely probing for a leftover spark.

Tony paused at the bend in the road and turned to face me. "Like I could forget." He closed the space between us. Overhead, chattering from a massive beech, a suicidal squirrel waved its tail like a red flag. Skippy perked and leaped, yanking the distracted Tony away from me, off the asphalt, and over a ditch. Barks and yelps and curses filled the valley. I took my time picking my way through weeds and rocks for a better view of the latest entertainment. Stretched to full length up against the mottled trunk, Skippy was the same height as Tony, who pulled with all his strength on the leash. The chittering rodent skittered branch to branch, scolding them both. The squirrel grew bored long before Skippy did. It had vaulted two trees over by the time Tony had the dog from hell controlled, soothed, chastised, and untangled once again.

And I laughed and laughed until I had to lean against the tree trunk, nerves shot, eyes watering. "Dog whisperer," I taunted, now playing with fire and hoping to get burned.

In two strides, Tony had me pinned against the tree. "You're the most infuriating woman I've ever met."

I should have felt a frission of fear, but all I felt was thrill. At least I was the most of something to someone. "Um, thank you?"

"You're bitchy, stubborn, mouthy—" and then he was kissing me and pressing my back into the smooth trunk, muttering words I blushed to hear in daylight. "That mouth," he murmured between kisses while a jealous Skippy tried to nose us apart.

I didn't feel like defending my mouth or any other part of my anatomy at that point, so I settled myself against the solid trunk and kissed back with heat, ignoring the dog, who tried to join in. Tony's face and neck glowed red by the time he came up for air. The leg I'd hooked around his waist and the hands I'd snaked under his shirt may have contributed to the change in temperature. It seemed I'd left all decorum behind in the churchyard. With a grind, I fanned the flames. The weather inside my sweats sweltered. His hand had slipped under the drawstring and was sliding towards my rear when we heard the beep.

"Get a room." The Prius prude couldn't have been much over eighteen, but the Main Line still operated by a different code, one the youth learned early. Skippy tugged. Tony groaned and rested his forehead against mine. "Not a bad idea," he said when the car disappeared around the curve.

"Cheesecake?" I pouted, half serious, half breathless.

The sigh he let out could've registered on a wind sock. "Give me a minute so I can stand up straight." I looked down and saw the problem, which really didn't seem all that big a problem to me. Not that it wasn't big.

"I could help you with that," I offered, summoning my sauciest smile. Even though it was rusty, it hit its mark. His eyes clouded.

"Nothing but trouble."

I no longer considered that an insult. Fates be damned. I deserved some fun.

CHAPTER TWENTY-ONE

Although a bona fide haunting can increase custom in hotels, restaurants, and saloons, not every business owner wants a haunting advertised. The sad fact is, ghosts can be bad for business.

The cheesecake came with cherries. Still in my perverse mood, I spooned a red globe slowly into my mouth and watched Tony's reaction. I don't know what had gotten into me, but I was going with it.

"Stop that. This is a family restaurant." The combination of annoyance and arousal on his face kept me motivated. I licked the spoon and fluttered my eyelashes. "Damn it, woman. If you don't cut that out, we're both going to be arrested."

"Mmm. Would they let us share a cell? Would we get handcuffs?" It was like my body had been hijacked by someone far more entertaining. I liked her.

Tony's eyes darkened. "Keep it up, Mary Catherine, and you won't get to finish that dessert." Of course, he'd wolfed down his apple pie within minutes, but I didn't bother to point that out.

Teasing, I took my time with the next spoonful. "And what would you substitute to satisfy my oral fixation?" In slow motion, I pulled the spoon from my mouth and then sucked it back in.

His look could burn through lead. Belligerently, he raked his eyes over me before staring me down. "Honey, once I start, I won't stop at…satisfaction."

Whoa—I'd stirred up more than I bargained for with that spoon. Outdone, I felt a flush creep up my chest and spread to my neck and face. My toes curled inside my impractical black pumps. Even chocolate swirl cheesecake couldn't compete with what Tony was cooking up, and he knew it. He grinned, knowing he'd won.

"More coffee?" The waitress bustled by, pot in hand, and without waiting for an answer, she topped off Tony's cup, splattering a few drops before slapping down the check.

Reality returned. In the chrome glare of the diner, all edges were sharp and mirrored. Across the lunch counter, I caught sight of myself, hair mussed, eyes wide and dilated, lips parted. My pink face clashed with my red sweater. Who was that untidy woman? I sat up straighter, smoothed my black slacks, and laid down the spoon. Back to business. "So…what's the posse's plan now?"

Tony took his time adding more cream. "That video's viral, so there's no way we can fight it." He picked up his fork to help himself to a bite from my plate. "It's all over the Internet now. And the Ghost Stalker's having a field day."

Visions of lawsuits danced in my head, and I felt like I'd choked down a tray of ice cubes. The sweater and the silk blouse beneath it did nothing to stop the chill in my gut. "Oh, crap. Look, will it help if I say that I'm horribly, incredibly, miserably sorry?"

He forked another bite. "No." While I balanced on the stool in limbo, he stirred his coffee and took a sip. "It's not just the show, Mary Catherine. A lot of people depend on a paycheck each week. People with kids. And mortgages." He finished the cup, frowning at the dregs. "But Peter came up with a spin that we think might work." The pause was maddening. "With Sylvie Blakely."

"You're using the medium? For God's sake, Tony, what are you thinking?

His smile turned bitter. "Peter's plan. We're having a séance. Filmed." He looked me in the eye. "Live. And before you get started, Mrs. Parrish loves the idea. It'll be like a séance anniversary, she says. Just like the good old days."

I stared back. "When?"

The smile turned to a grimace. "When else? Halloween."

I panicked. "Tony, you can't do this. Do you know how many things are floating around that place? And down the hill in the cemetery? Jesus, it'll be like ringing a dinner bell." I leaned over and grabbed his arm. "Listen to me, damn it." He looked down at my hand and then up at me. I pulled away first.

With his napkin, he wiped dribbles of coffee off the counter. "It's already done, Mary Catherine. The show must go on. And in the meantime, I have to scope out next month's location." He picked up the check and tucked the tip under his saucer. "It'll be a nice change—a dull plumbing supply place in the Northeast off Roosevelt Boulevard." His face lit up a few watts. "Hey, how about riding with me to check it out? Like, you know, give me a head's up, just in case?" Maddeningly, he had the same look on his face that Skippy wore when Peter dangled treats.

"What—just in case it really is haunted?"

His smile turned grim again. "You got it. Forewarned is forearmed and all that." With that parting shot, he headed for the cashier.

Everything in me screamed to run back to my relatively safe, predictable existence. But Tony had those melting chocolate eyes and that dimple and those big, warm hands. And he understood about cheesecake. I tried to seem nonchalant as I held open the door. "Sure. Why not?" My voice was only a little shaky.

* * *

The late afternoon sunlight cast long shadows when he parked the van at the Northeast Philly site. Since it was Sunday, traffic was lighter on the boulevard behind us, but the air still hung thick with the pall of exhaust and rattle of trucks. Before us hulked an ugly concrete warehouse built for function instead of aesthetics. The leprous white brick monstrosity next door seemed to have the same design-challenged architect. "Sure you're up for this, Mary?" Tony looked a little guilty, which cheered me up some.

I took a deep, noxious breath as I slid out of the van. "Hey, what could happen? We're at in an industrial district in a heavily populated area on a sunny day. Hardly ghost territory." I laughed nervously.

"The guy's meeting us on the showroom side. Uh—" He glanced at his notes. "Brian O'Toole." He kissed my cheek. "Ready?"

I'm ashamed to admit that the slight peck perked me up. Pitiful. I nodded, tracking Tony like a lost kitten through the parking lot, past the loading zone, and around the side of the warehouse. The showroom side was marginally more inviting. "O'Toole Plumbing and Heating Supply, est. 1964, Kitchen and Bath Showroom," the sign announced. Someone back in the seventies had built a storefront with diagonal wood siding and a mansard roof. It would've been out of place anywhere, but it looked even odder squatting next to the stark three-story structure that dominated it on one side.

152

A wiry figure in a windbreaker stood smoking by the showroom's smudged glass door. As the wind stirred strands of his thin, sandy hair, he turned up his collar and huddled more deeply into the doorway. He flicked the butt away and reached out a hand when Tony approached.

"Tony, man, thanks for not coming by during business hours." Up close, the owner could have been anywhere from forty to sixty, given his taut, lined face and receding hairline. He nodded at me, blue eyes troubled and suspicious.

Tony returned the handshake. "Yeah, Brian, I get that. Ghosts and clogged drains don't mix." He dragged me closer. "This is my...friend, Mary. She couldn't resist the chance to ride shotgun on this." I cringed at the way he said *friend*. Maybe that's all I was to him, after all. A friend with benefits.

Although Brian laughed, the tension didn't leave his bony shoulders. "Hey, not my idea of a good time, but to each his own." He sorted through his key ring, selected two, and opened the door. "Come on in. I'll take you around." He punched in the code for the alarm and flipped on the lights. "We're keeping this all low key, right? I don't want to get my men more worked up than they already are."

Tony nodded. "Remember, we're here to prove there's nothing to worry about."

It was as if Brian hadn't heard him. He smoothed his hair against his freckled scalp and cleared his throat before he answered. "They're really freaked out. I'm hoping if you guys look into it and don't find anything, they'll lay off and things will get back to normal."

The showroom boasted an arsenal of pipes and fixtures gleaming metallically under the track lights. As we wove our way around the displays, I braced for that awful tingle and dreadful clamminess, but it never came. Computers, file cabinets, advertising posters, and display notebooks crowded the tiny, airless office, but nothing lethal lurked under the desks. Relieved, I relaxed a fraction, leaning on a desk to ease the pinch of my too-high heels.

"We haven't had trouble in here," Brian admitted as he led the way to the rear of the building. "It's out back that they're complaining."

In the echoing warehouse, the smell of machine oil and diesel mixed with something more acrid — nothing tangible or clearly identifiable, but definitely unsettling. I instinctively drew back, wrinkled my nose, and wished for hand sanitizer. "Here's where the problem is," Brian explained, gesturing to the pallets and crates behind him. "The men won't come in here alone anymore." Most of the shadows had vanished when Brian turned on the lights, but the yawning space retained a dark feel even under the buzz of the fluorescents. Once Brian walked away, I pulled Tony aside to warn him.

Tony's brows contracted. "Did you see anything?"

I took my time answering, eyes flickering from corner to corner. "No. No, that's not it. There isn't anyone here." I turned around in a circle. "That's not the problem." I was starting to break out in a cold sweat as I searched for an exit.

Oblivious, Tony smiled the first genuine smile I'd seen in hours. "That's the only good news I've had all day." He put an arm around me. "Looks like we're clear to debunk, then. Thank God for small favors." He gave me a quick squeeze before letting go and shouting across the concrete vault. "Yo, Brian, it looks good. I'll give you a call tomorrow to iron out the details." He waved and strode across the loading dock to the van, where he relaxed until I caught up. "Thanks, Mary Catherine. I mean it. You were a big help."

What a fucking numbskull he was. The Fates nodded in agreement.

"Don't thank me too fast, Tony." The whiplash tone finally snapped him to attention. I admit that a mean piece of me enjoyed watching his expression shift from placable to pole-axed. "Yeah, it's clean." I crossed my arms and wrapped them around myself as I stared over his shoulder, trying to keep the bile down. "But you'll want to stay away from that building next door. Really. Far. Away."

CHAPTER TWENTY-TWO

"Shiiiiit." Tony stretched out the obscenity so that it had extra vowels. "Peter's going to go ballistic over this one." He opened his phone. "You're sure, right?" He noticed my expression. "Stupid question. Of course you're sure."

"If you stay in the front part, in the showroom, you should be okay," I ventured. "That part's safe. I think. Probably." I nodded as if wishing could make it so.

The van rocked slightly as he leaned against it, still texting. "Just when I thought things might be getting better, you drop another bomb."

That got my back up. "Hey, I didn't do anything. I'm just along for the cheesecake, remember? And let me tell you, it's a damn long time between bites." While a cold wind tossed a plastic bag into the air, we traded glares.

"You're right." Tony reached behind me to open the van door without dropping his gaze. "Maybe we're both in need of a bite or two."

I contemplated multiple interpretations of his remark while huddling in my seat trying to get warm. Through the windshield, I watched shadows stretch like fingers across the parking lot as Tony ground the gears. The sky had shifted from dusty rose to purple by the time we drove past the neon sign for the Mayfair Diner. Since we didn't even slow down, I gathered food wasn't on the menu again any time soon.

Some silences are comfortable, even companionable — words aren't necessary, because all the blanks are already filled in. This wasn't one of those silences. Between us the dead air sizzled. Prickly and wired, I stared at my reflection in the window, feeling the tension buzz around me. The buzz coalesced and concentrated near my hip.

Of course. D.J. When I had stopped by Grey Crag to change clothes, I'd told him to check in. Hoping he hadn't wreaked any additional havoc, I pulled the vibrating phone from my pocket. "Hey, kiddo, you alive? Is the house still standing? Did Peter pick up Skippy? Did you bother Mrs. Parrish? Has anyone served a summons?" Tony looked over and shook his head.

"Obviously, yeah, yeah, not much, and…what's a summons?" D.J.'s mouth must have been full, judging by the muffled response.

"Never mind. I take it you found yourself some *dinner*?" I glared once more at Tony, who kept his eyes on the road.

"Mom, as a public service, I'm depleting the dangerous stockpile of leftovers in the refrigerator. And for dessert, I can always eat the chocolate off Zina's altar."

"Just stay out of the bottles. And pack up your stuff for tomorrow. You know how you drag on Monday mornings."

"I hate school," he mumbled. I rested my head against the cold glass, tired of hearing it.

"I know, but it's a necessary evil. Like taking a shower. And D.J., no computer, remember?" Tony looked over at the mention of computers.

"But there's a zombie show I want to watch."

"So? You've seen it. More than once. I don't know what your fascination is with those shows, anyway."

"It would so rock if I lived in a zombie world. I'd be awesome. And I wouldn't have to go to that stupid school. I could just do whatever I want."

"Right. As long as you could outrun your neighbors. Anyway, kiddo, behave yourself, at least until I get back. I should be home in...?" I looked over at Tony, who was concentrating on merging into heavier traffic.

Tony turned his head and looked back, jaw set. "Tell him it'll be late."

* * *

The van bumped over potholes and patched asphalt, past stone and brick duplexes, past churches and motels and office buildings, heading to the river and the expressway.

I remembered this cityscape. "We're going the wrong way." At the junction, we should have steered towards the Main Line exits. "Tony, hold on. You're going into the city." Up ahead, around the bend of the Schuylkill River, the art museum loomed. "You can exit up here and turn around," I offered.

"Anyone ever mention you have control issues?"

Well, yes, but not lately. "Just trying to help." I packed as much sarcasm as I could into the words.

He glanced away from the traffic to consider my answer. "Maybe that's part of the problem."

"What do you mean by that?" I thought only David could get me so riled so fast.

He switched lanes before answering. "You don't have to feel responsible for everything, you know. It's not like the fate of the free world rests on your shoulders."

"I never said it did. But the fate of my dinner does, and you're headed in the wrong direction."

He smiled like a stray dog with a stolen hot dog. "I guess that remains to be seen."

So we were going to a restaurant after all. I looked down at my wrinkled slacks and wondered if I had lipstick and a comb in my purse. "Am I dressed all right for whatever eatery you're kidnapping me to?"

He took a few seconds to look me over when we stopped at a traffic signal. "A little overdressed, actually."

So it was probably some South Philly sports bar. Maybe I could make do with a burger and cheese fries. But despite my pointed comments and helpful directions to Center City, Tony persisted on his misdirected course. He drove past the museum to Spring Garden, finally braking in front of a rosy brick house that was better suited to nineteenth century Paris than twenty-first century Philadelphia. "We're here," he announced.

I looked up and down a residential block. "Where's 'here'?"

He took excessive care undoing his seatbelt. "My place."

The world stopped turning for a second. "Oh." Tony set the emergency brake, gathered his papers and phone, and walked around the van to the passenger side.

"Coming?" When I stepped down, he seemed taller.

Behind him, the dark house sat apart from its neighbor, hemmed in by a wrought iron fence. It was one of the few detached dwellings in the eclectic, upscale neighborhood — not the kind of place I'd imagined he lived in at all. It looked more Victor Hugo than Mario Puzo. All it needed was gaslight and an urchin.

"Well?" He shifted impatiently.

"I'm thinking."

Exasperated, he tugged me towards him and slammed the van door behind me, locking it. "You think too much, Mary Catherine." As he pulled me up the steps, I tilted my head back to get the full effect of his home. It stood three stories high, the crenellated roof-line and hooded gables sharp against the evening sky.

"Nice digs."

Tony grunted as he struggled to unlock the first set of glass doors. "Works for me." He opened the second set of doors and looked back. "I thought you were hungry." Turning, he walked into the narrow hallway, switching on the lights. My heels tapped hollowly after him.

Sometime in the eighties, a misguided soul must have tried to renovate. The peach paint and brass lighting fixtures looked ludicrous in a space that cried for Tiffany and draperies. But the bones were good—high ceilings, deep alcoves, carved molding, walnut woodwork.

"Kitchen's this way." We crossed through a living room lit only by outside street lamps, and I had a fleeting glimpse of grungy bachelor furniture, a tangle of computer components, and a leggy, languishing date palm. The kitchen was worse—modular white cabinets and an uneasy mix of appliances that looked neither utilitarian nor vintage. But it was clean.

"I eat out a lot." Tony must have gathered something from my expression.

I nodded towards the refrigerator. "Any chance there's a frozen cheesecake in there?"

He smiled. "Don't worry. I shopped. You'll have plenty to eat." In record time, he hauled cheese and prosciutto from the deli drawer, grapes from a bowl, bread, a knife, napkins, and a bottle of Chianti from the butcher block counter. "Grab a couple of wine glasses from that shelf behind you."

"What, no fava beans?"

He laughed, and I relaxed a degree. "Get that corkscrew next to you, too."

"How long have you lived here?" I reached for the shelf.

"I bought it at the end of last season. Haven't had a chance to do much with it yet."

"It's big. For one person, I mean."

The corner of his mouth turned up. "I like to spread out." He sliced the bread and offered it to me with a piece of cheese. "And there's plenty of room for the family when they come around. And stay. Sometimes for days, but waddaya gonna do?"

This was a new side of Tony: expansive, relaxed, at home in his castle. I wandered back into the hall, noticing the series of abstract black and white photos hung along its length. "Did you take these?"

He stood behind me, peering over my shoulder. "Yeah, a few years ago. Around the city. That one's South Street. This one's from the Italian market."

"You like city life. You must, to see it this way."

He shrugged. "Every place has something. One reason I picked this place is it's one of a kind. And it's solid, you know?" He slapped the plaster wall.

I did know. People's homes were like extensions of themselves. Insanely curious, I peered up the staircase, wondering where he slept. "It's beautiful, Tony. Really."

"Glad you like it." He sounded serious. Deftly, he arranged the impromptu feast on the chrome coffee table in front of the sofa. As I gaped at the magnitude of the spread, he chuckled. "Heard you had an appetite. Make yourself at home, Mary." Tony took his time uncorking the wine and pouring it into the glasses.

I sank into the lumpy sofa, feeling as if some beast had swallowed me. I wasn't sure I'd be able to extricate myself later and couldn't decide if that bothered me or not.

"Drink up. You'll feel better." He'd been watching me, amused. I tossed my head in what I hoped was a confident gesture and reached for the glass he held out.

Our fingers touched when I accepted the wine. "I'm fine." Inwardly, I cringed at my squeaky tone. "So…you like this? This kind of wine, I mean?"

Tony reached up to tuck a hank of hair behind my ear. "Full bodied. Smooth." His fingertips caressed my cheek. As I held my breath, he leaned over and kissed the spot he'd touched. "Lingering aftertaste." He waggled his brows. "What's not to like?" When he trailed his lips down, nibbling the line of my jaw, I remembered the way he'd lapped the spilled drops the last night we spent together. Now I was breathing again, all hot and bothered and embarrassed for fear he knew what I was thinking and was laughing at me. The wine shook in the glass.

"Stop it." Tony's eyes narrowed, and he took the glass from me. "Stop thinking so much."

"I can't help it. My brain doesn't have an 'off' switch."

"Neither does your mouth, but we can fix that. Here. Eat this." He held out a thick slice of Italian bread mounded with provolone and prosciutto. I bit.

Tony was right. Food makes everything better. I chewed slowly. Swallowed. "It's good. Thanks." I savored the second bite. And the third, and then another slice and some grapes. Stalling. "So…what do you do in your free time?"

The laugh burst from him. "Are you kidding?"

"No. I really want to know. When you're not ghost hunting, what do you do?"

He scratched the back of his neck. "Paperwork."

"Oh, come on, Tony. You must do something besides work."

"I do you," he added. "As of Friday."

He really needed an intervention before he stuck that foot any farther down his throat. "Besides that." I sipped the dry wine, needing a boost.

"Okay..." He hooked his arms behind his head and stretched his feet out in front of him. "I catch an Eagles game now and then. Go down to the rec center and help out with the kids' leagues. Hit Happy Hour once a week or so with guys from my old neighborhood. Take Ma to mass."

"That's so sweet. I like a guy who's good to his mama." The wine tasted sweeter the more I drank.

He grinned. "She wouldn't have it any other way. Her and my sisters, they keep me in line."

"So no other women?" He just didn't strike me as the celibate type.

Tony looked uncomfortable and shifted around on the sofa. "Well, you know, I'm no saint. But nothing that lasted. Girls from the neighborhood. Women on shoots. My last girlfriend ended up getting married. Just not to me." He couldn't quite hide the hurt in his eyes.

My heart contracted a touch. I reached out and took his hand. "Her loss," I said lightly. "She obviously failed to appreciate your manly charms." Just remembering some of those charms had me heating up again. I finished the glass and set it down as Tony leaned in. This time, he went straight for my mouth. The kiss started out gentle, deepening until I was pressed against the sofa cushions, gradually sliding further down until somehow I found myself wedged in and not minding at all. My eyes drifted shut.

"Open up." His voice was low, the thrum of an engine. He kissed each lid. "I want to see you." And he held me with his eyes as he traced the curve of my hip, the contour of my waist, the shape of my breasts. Now I knew exactly why a rabbit froze when a predator was near. The pull of danger was like a snare. So was the pleasure. He pressed a kiss to my forehead and eased back.

"Wanna see the rest of the house? We can have dessert upstairs."

I nodded, not trusting my voice, and he gathered the remaining dishes, including a plate piled with chunks of a chewy candy Tony called *torrone*. Carrying the wine, I followed him and the remainder of the food to the upper level, where a jumble of doors beckoned. "Over here." Tony stood in front of the one open door.

I was halfway into the space before I realized where we were headed. Okay, I had an inkling that the upstairs level included the bedrooms, but I thought that maybe there was a kind of a sitting room or something up there, maybe with a TV. I thought we'd eat more and kind of ease back into things. In this room, the only place to sit was the bed.

CHAPTER TWENTY-THREE

Internet Chat Room:

To answer your question, since we know that raw emotion can linger as a residual haunting, it may be possible that extreme emotional states in the present can and do heighten paranormal activity.

It was a huge, inviting bed—serviceable, sturdy, its rounded posts and solid double-paneled headboard made of oak. The thick king mattress took up much of the floor space, barely leaving room for a dresser and bedside table, where Tony laid out the food. Covers had been pulled up, but I wouldn't have called the bed made. Unbidden, an image of Tony, naked and sexy under those covers, flashed in my mind, and I teetered somewhere between anxious and tantalized. "Pretty sure of yourself, aren't you?" I kept my voice Bacall-cool and crossed my arms over my breast, still clutching the wine stems and bottle.

For a few agonizing seconds, my appetite and my reason grappled. There was more than dessert up for grabs here. There was self-respect. Dignity, even. But if that night in my bed had been an appetizer and the interlude downstairs was the second course, I was curious about the menu options for the last. Reason was nudged out of the ring. Battling shyness, I set down my burden and strode towards the bed, which looked soft and yielding, in contrast to my stiff and awkward self.

Tony bounced and patted the space beside him. Gingerly, I perched on the edge, legs primly together, but at least I stopped myself from folding my hands in my lap. What was I, a first grader? If this was a seduction, I was decades out of practice, still stinging from our previous encounter in my room. And which underwear was I wearing? Not the cotton flowered ones, I hoped. My forehead wrinkled as I tried to remember the quick change earlier.

"Here," he said, reaching over and popping a nougat in my mouth. It melted on my tongue. "Wash it down," he added filling my glass and handing it to me. His breath caught when I brushed against his arm, and I faltered, jostling the wine.

"Oh. Excuse me." Welcoming the distraction, I stretched for a napkin and vigorously blotted at the spill on the bedspread, figuring this act of clumsiness would be enough to convince any man I was a lost cause. "I'm so sorry. I hope it won't stain."

"Mary Catherine, you're killing me here." Increasingly, it struck me that I was sprawled across his lap, and the rocking motion had definitely caused a reaction. Now I wasn't the only one who was stiff.

I jumped up. "Oh, God, Tony, I—"

He rose beside me and covered my mouth with his. He tasted of wine and temptation— tangy, compelling. Tilting my head to deepen the kiss, I eased closer, arching as he stroked my back. I linked an arm around his neck, thoroughly enthralled. We were both breathless when we came up for air.

I reached behind him to set down the empty glass. His hands lingered on my backside, following its curve. I practically purred at the sensation.

"So…fast or slow?"

"Huh?" I paused, looking over my shoulder. "What'd you say?" He wrapped his arms around me, and I leaned back and nestled against the length of him. "This is so nice, Tony."

"Mary Catherine," he prodded.

"Mmm?" The wine and kiss had muddled my thinking. "What?"

"We're skating on icicles here. How do you want it? Because soon, there won't be a choice."

"Oh." I chewed my lip. "It can't be both?"

His voice was strained. "You have a lot of confidence in me."

I turned. His eyes really did have lovely gold flecks floating in the irises, I noticed. "Enormous confidence." I slid my hand down the placket of his white shirt, over his belly, past his belt to his crotch and squeezed, watching his eyes turn to slits. "Enormous."

He'd backed me up against the wall between the table and the bed before I uttered the last syllable. Desire came whip-sharp. "Fast it is, then," he growled, pulling my sweater and blouse over my head, reaching down to peel off the bra and burying his face between my breasts. His hands slid down my rib cage and around the waistband of my slacks, tugging hard at the zipper. Under his busy mouth, my breasts swelled and heart pounded. My slacks slid off. Trailing a line of heat, his mouth dropped down past my collarbone, nipping the underside of a breast, moving lower. I ran my hands over his broad back. Gasped.

Barely, I retained enough presence of mind to look where his black curls hovered. Thank God, I had the red panties on — the string bikinis that matched the bra. And nothing else but those high heels.

"This seems a little — unequal," I whispered. "I'm feeling kind of naked here." He stood back up and pressed his forehead to mine while he opened his fly. "Honey, if I wait any longer, we'll both be sorry."

My knees gave way when he yanked the panties to one side and pressed his cock against me. "Hold on just a second." He jerked the words out, reaching towards the bedside table.

"You need more to eat? Now?"

"Got a Happy Meal right here," he mumbled, dipping his head to nuzzle my neck.

"Such a sweet talker. How do the ladies ever resist you?"

"You're pretty irresistible yourself. You drive me crazy. Right to the edge." He nuzzled lower. "But I do need — " and he opened the drawer and thumped a box of condoms onto the bed — "some peace of mind."

I looked sideways at the size of the box. "That's a lot of serenity."

"You're the one who gave the big vote of confidence."

I grinned. "How many come in a box?"

The grin he returned was strained. "Enough."

"You sure about that?"

"Let's find out." He ripped open the package and tossed the strip of condoms on the bedspread. Grabbing one, he tore it with his teeth and sheathed himself, then paused.

"Mary Catherine."

"Tony."

"Hang on." So much for finesse. And I forgot all about complaining when he drove inside me, pushing, then withdrawing, each time deeper. He clasped me in thick arms, flattening my chest with his, frantically seeking my mouth. Caught in the frenzy, I locked my leg around his waist and gave in to rough pleasure, rocking, swallowing his groans and meeting each thrust. The wine glasses shook with our coupling. Needing an anchor, I grabbed his hips and held on. My thighs trembled uncontrollably by the time he let out a shout, shuddering against me for so long I wondered if I'd have to call 911.

So...that was fast, I mused as he panted, still pinning me to the wall. Up against the wall. Another first. David had been way too tall to manage this. While my insides throbbed with pent-up pleasure, my heartbeat slowed. Tentatively, I flexed and reveled in the friction. In bliss, I slid fully down on him again, striving for my own release. At that, Tony lifted his head. He looked like he'd been hit by a truck.

"Hey, remember me?" I asked and scraped my teeth against his salty neck.

His voice was hoarse. "Give me just a second."

He was still hard. I ground against him once more, frustration building.

I could feel him grit his teeth at the stimulation, but my own discomfort bordered on pain. "Hold on, Mary." He retreated a few inches, leaving me spread-eagled and seething.

"Tony. Don't stop. Please."

And Tony stopped to listen. Below, the doorbell rang again.

"Must be Peter," he grumbled, withdrawing his fingers from where he'd started to stroke me to strip off the condom, zip, and buckle. He kissed me hard. "Hold that thought. You know I gotta get this." Unsteady, I leaned against the wall as he tucked his shirt into his khakis and wiped his hand on a discarded towel. And he walked out the door, leaving it wide open. The way he left my mouth.

I was staring at the line of foil packets snaking across the bedspread when a cold nose between my legs brought me completely to my senses. "Bad dog. No. Go away." I shoved at the massive head and clamped my legs together, tamping down a murderous impulse by reminding myself that Skippy wasn't the real dog in this situation. Then I set about dressing.

Ignoring Skippy's attack on the remaining bread and cheese, I yanked up my damp panties, stepped into my slacks, and looked around for the rest of my clothes. After a cursory search, I gave up the bra as a lost cause. Eventually, I found my blouse and sweater inside out in the far corner. I discovered the bathroom — a decorator's nightmare of cracked tile, rust-stained porcelain, and curling linoleum. The toilet was missing its seat. At least the water was hot.

The hallway made a perfect megaphone, so I had no trouble overhearing the conversation from below as I pulled myself back together.

"You have her lined up, right? Sylvie says we need her if we want to pull this séance thing off."

"I'm working on it, man. Give me a little time. She's the type that needs careful handling." *Something you apparently aren't capable of*, I thought gripping the doorknob so hard that my hand hurt.

"I take it you're *handling* her just fine." I could hear the snark in Peter's voice even a floor away. "I hope better than you handled that kid of hers. Do you know the video's up to 50,000 hits?"

"We'll get that straightened out too. The show can still come out on top here." The next few words were muffled. "Just a few more to cover."

My irate heels tapped a warning, so neither man bothered to look up when I entered the living room. They stood close under a dim chandelier, heads bent over a sheaf of papers, while Peter talked. "So the promos are set for the special and I lined up this panel of experts. We can film them downtown in the studio in the morning, get those segments in the can early. That way we can focus on the meat. We're not buried yet, Tony."

"I gotta switch out a couple of those cameras. Maybe add more lights before Halloween. We'll only get one shot at this." Tony ran his fingers through his hair.

"Speaking of getting one shot," I hissed at Tony as I slipped past him. "I'm just grabbing my purse. Don't let me interrupt anything important." I prayed I could get a cab to come to this part of town at night.

Peter looked up from his papers, head tilted. Despite my mood, I wanted to giggle at the pose, so like Skippy's. Instead, I nodded once at him. There was still the matter of a potential lawsuit with D.J. "Peter."

He nodded back. "Mrs. Livingston." And I would've escaped to the kitchen before he said more if Skippy hadn't trotted in, triumphantly bearing my red bra. Peter's expression shifted from puzzlement to amusement. Skippy, bless his heart, just wagged. "Missing something?" Peter arched a perfect blond eyebrow.

Unwilling to lose another shred of my threadbare dignity, I crossed my arms and stonewalled. "Nope. Not a thing." By then, Skippy had dropped the bra and was tugging on the elastic strap with his teeth while holding the cups down with his paws. Through the whole exchange, Tony had wisely kept quiet, but when the elastic snapped, so did he.

He had the gall to laugh.

Chapter Twenty-Four

Castration, then boiling in oil, I thought, warming to the idea. *Extra virgin olive oil. With the whole thing captured on video so I could replay it again and again and again. Using his own damn cameras.*

The vision helped block out the depressing fact that I was alone in a lumpy bed with nothing to distract me but ugly wallpaper and my brutal fantasies.

At least they gave me more satisfaction than Tony had. And here I'd thought he was the antithesis of what I'd left behind. The package may be different, but underneath he was just another David.

"Fuck." I threw my pillow against the wall and rolled out of bed. I wasn't going to get any more sleep. What was wrong with me? Why did I attract these loathsome, self-centered guys? Was I a loser magnet? Why did I let them use me? Would no one ever cherish me for me?

And where had my brain gone last night?

I replayed the entire fateful day and concluded that I was a pitiful mark just waiting to be "handled" by the first guy to crook a finger. In my mind, I assembled a checklist for putting my life back in order. I needed to swear off wine, men, and intimate dinners if I ever expected a peaceful and productive future. I could live without sex. Lots of people did. The Dali Lama. Lady Gaga. Isaac Newton. Jane Austen. Some of the Jonas Brothers. Emily Dickinson. A vibrant, creative life without sex was possible.

If only I could think of something else. Peace through Zen. Great literature. Apples. Cookies. Shortbread cookies in the pantry—phallic towers of cookies just waiting to be swallowed. Once the image took hold, I was powerless to resist. Swathed in my flannel robe, I braved the dark halls. Six cookies later, I felt better. Not exactly satisfied, but better.

By the time Zina arrived in the early morning, I'd eaten the entire sleeve and was sipping my second cup of doctored tea, liberally laced with liquor and sugar. It didn't sweeten me up. Since I was staring back at my mother's picture and plotting variations of Tony's demise, the sour mood was understandable.

"What is this doing in my pantry?" Zina held the offending Tupperware full of ashes at arm's length. I debated before answering.

"Urn broke." Short. Clear. Direct. "Want some tea? There's more in the pot." I gestured with the mug.

Zina set down the tote bag she carried and peeled off her coat. "You have been up to something," she accused. It wasn't a question.

"Not anymore." I contemplated another cookie. She snatched the package from me and placed it back on the shelf.

"You had enough." She sat opposite me and waited.

"Sorry about the ashes. I cleaned up what I could."

"These things, they happen. But when they happen, when what was quiet wakes, then comes trouble." She looked at the altar behind me. "You got trouble?"

"Yeah, you could say that." I couldn't quite keep the quaver from my voice. I was a gullible, overweight, frumpy single mother in a dead-end job, dependent on a dotty old lady, fucked over by an opportunistic geek, and haunted by a slew of ghastly ghosts, most of whom I didn't even know. *Present company excepted, Mom.* I lifted my mug in salute.

Zina planted her fists on her hips and glared. Her disapproval was thicker than her eyebrows. "That bottle. It was for your mother."

"She said she didn't mind sharing under the circumstances." I paused to gulp some more forgetfulness. "See, I'd had a shitty day." And then I did the unthinkable. I told Zina about it. She listened impassively until I recounted the rousing argument on the sidewalk when Tony paid off the cab and insisted on taking me back to Grey Crag.

"Hmm." She pursed her lips.

"Hmm?"

"He did the right thing, driving you back. They both, they are not bad men. They act *tonto,* stupid, but..."

Stupid didn't begin to cover it. Tony had railed from Spring Garden to the expressway about how dim-witted *I* was to consider taking a cab all the way to the Main Line. While he sped past several exits, he justified his decision to leave me hanging in order to answer the door and plan the next program with Peter. He didn't mention the fact that he was just sleeping with me to clear the way for the séance.

We were within five miles of the mansion before he registered that I had nothing to say to him. By then, his grudging apology was a textbook example of too little, too late. He committed the ultimate sin, though, when he tried to kiss me good night and recapture some of the heat he'd enjoyed so completely. But winter had come, and I left him out in the cold.

I hoped his cock froze, turned black, and fell off.

Zina didn't even blink when I said as much, but she did take the bottle away and suggest D.J. catch the bus this one time. She also revealed an unexpected human side by explaining to Mrs. Parrish and D.J. that I wasn't feeling well and needed to stay in bed for the morning. Of course, bed had all sorts of associations, so instead of resting, I ended up stripping the sheets and then sinking into the mound on the floor to cry.

What was wrong with me? I never cried. I stopped crying when I was twelve. I hadn't cried when my father died. Or when I found the Visa bill with David's hotel charges on it. But here I sat, wailing into a pile of sheets and pillowcases. In just a weekend, I'd been reduced to a quivering mass of self-pity, whining like a kicked puppy. God, I disgusted myself.

When my cell phone buzzed, I welcomed the interruption. I should have been suspicious when I didn't recognize the number.

It was Tony.

CHAPTER TWENTY-FIVE

From Sylvie Blakely's 'Other World' Web Site

I'm pleased to offer an easy way for you to get my Level One Aura Reading to determine which type of Chakra Energizing or Aura Cleansing you may need. Just send a recent photo and $49.95, and I will begin assessing your vibrational level in order to reveal, renew, and revitalize you.

"Mary, don't hang up." How did he know I already had my thumb on the button? "Tried calling from my cell, but I couldn't get through," he continued. Of course not. I'd blocked his number before I had even stepped out of my shoes the night before. "Come on, Mary Catherine. This is important. It's about the séance."

Tears on hold, I projected enough venom to drop an elephant. "You've got thirty seconds. What about it?"

"Honey, I have to talk to you."

Though I heard the plea, I was coiled for a strike. "Talk. But just about the séance."

"How about I pick you up—"

"Never again." Oh, that sneaky, sleazy little technosexual. "Séance?"

"Okay, if that's the way you want to play it." He might have smothered a sigh, but I didn't care. "Sylvie needs a session with you before the taping."

"Didn't realize that the polar icecaps were reforming in hell."

"Mrs. Parrish said you — and I'm quoting here — would be more than happy to participate." A chilly silence followed before he added, "Since you know how much this means to her."

His underhanded tactics knew no bounds, apparently. Here he was *handling* me again. I snorted. The bastard. He'd never really cared about me. I was a means to an end, with maybe a few detours just for fun.

"We'll pay you." He sounded exasperated.

I let the silence stretch before answering. "Define 'session.'" Sylvie wasn't going to lure me into her less-than-lively chat room for any price. I had enough trouble keeping that world on the sidelines as it was, not to mention the upcoming threat of uninvited guests at the séance. But the session Tony outlined was more of a brief meeting that Sylvie wanted to conduct with all the participants — something about reading their auras or feeling their energy. I thought of the size of my credit card bill and wavered.

"How much?" I liked the idea of making him pay for the betrayal and humiliation I was suffering. When he named the sum, I wavered some more. "I might be available sometime this week, for Mrs. Parrish's sake. But I have some conditions."

"Name 'em." Tony was all business now.

"I'm not rehashing any of my past. I'm not talking to anything she might drag in out of the darkness. And most important —"

"Yeah?"

180

"When she comes for the interview, you don't come with her. I can stand seeing chirpy Ashley or even Peter, but not you."

I could barely hear him when he accepted the terms.

* * *

Zina and Peter were sparring in the entryway later that week while Sylvie Blakely drifted along the wall, studying portraits and artifacts at random. When I paused on the landing, she looked up, and her whifty expression dissolved to something akin to shock. Not quite the reaction I liked to elicit, but if it kept her at a distance, all the better. After I reached her side, though, she continued to focus on the landing. Scowling, I realized she must see the grim piñata that had been haunting me since my first day here. Maybe I had to reevaluate my opinion of her ability. And a good medium was a bad omen.

Skippy bounded from Zina's side to reacquaint himself with my crotch. Scratching his ears idly, I tuned in to enjoy the newest spat between his two favorite people. Who needed TV? This time, Zina was haranguing Peter about the need to exercise the poor *perro* so that Skippy didn't take off across the fields whenever a door opened. Peter, as usual, remained cowed and attentive. As she scolded, she stepped progressively closer until her chest bumped his midsection, and she had to crane her neck to skewer him with her heated black gaze. At the contact, Peter's lips quirked up. He made no effort to lean out of the line of fire. I wondered if he encouraged Skippy to misbehave just to get Zina to yell at him. She seemed to relish the passionate exchange as much as he did. So kinky.

"Mrs. Livingston?" Sylvie seemed pale, but since the bloodless look was her signature style, I couldn't tell for sure if she was reacting to the gruesome interior decorations at

Grey Crag or just displaying her natural pallor. "Tony said you were open to talking with me. Could we go someplace, um, quieter?"

I consulted my mental list of safe spots and led her to the library. That haven harbored new hazards, however. Seated snugly on the brocade sofa, coffee and baked goods spread out before them, Mrs. Parrish and Tony pored over yet another scrapbook. I stopped short at the door, ambushed by the spurt of happiness that escaped when I saw him. He'd cleaned up for the occasion, by his standards, at least, wearing pressed grey slacks and a blue oxford shirt that stretched a bit across the belly.

Despite our agreement, he'd come back, hoping to wear me down or ply me with presents, perhaps. Could it be that he missed me? I braced myself to resist.

"Here's one from that year," Mrs. Parrish was saying. "Don't you love the gowns? Just look at this one—it's a Lanvin. Taffeta, I should think. You don't see beading like that nowadays."

"So no other pictures from the night of the séance? We were planning to recreate as much as possible." Tony took the scrapbook into his lap to examine it more closely, and one black curl tumbled over his forehead. I remembered how soft it felt from the night before when it brushed my stomach.

Maybe I wouldn't make him beg too much.

When I cleared my throat, they looked up. "Tony. Didn't expect to see you." There. Offhand. Not too inviting, but I'd given him a chance to start groveling.

So I was surprised when he nodded a greeting and said, in a formal tone I hadn't heard for weeks, "Mrs. Livingston, Sylvie. I was hoping to speak with Mrs. Parrish alone. Would you mind?"

It probably took me a few seconds to school my expression so it revealed nothing. "I'm so sorry we interrupted. We'll just move to the dining room. Will that be all for now, Mrs. Parrish?" The apology stuck in my throat. I coughed again.

She nodded regally. "And if you would take this tray on to the kitchen on your way?"

I thought of several answers, every one of which would cost me a job. So I just picked up the tray, snatching Tony's cup of coffee and half-finished muffin away before he finished. I left the mess on the counter for Zina to find when she finished her tango with Peter.

Sylvie floated after me, gasping at the sight of pink and green sugar skulls grinning from the altar, shying away from the plastic tub of cremains, but refraining from comment until we reached the dining room. She shut the double doors behind her and leaned against them. "How do you stand it?" she rasped. "It's much worse than it was a week ago." Though the room was warm, she wrapped her skinny arms around her ribcage and shivered.

I ignored the faint tapping in the walls that began as soon as we entered the space. "No idea what you're talking about." I kept my voice even and watched the dust motes float in a stray beam of sunlight. Zina must've given up cleaning in here too.

If I were honest, the undead residents didn't bother me nearly as much as the callous cretin in the library.

"Right. You see nothing." She dismissed my answer with a sniff. "It's all over you. Violet. Gold. Pulsing. Distorted." She shook her head to erase the vision. "So strong. No wonder they find you." Drawn to the window, she basked in the radiant heat like the coldblooded creature I suspected her to be. When you hang around dead people, some of their corruption's bound to rub off. "Tony mentioned you discovered a presence at the plumbing business?"

I wanted to tread very carefully here. "The showroom's fine."

"And the warehouse?"

I took a deep breath. "Iffy." Conscience demanded more. "I'd skip that location if I were you."

She nodded slowly. "I'll talk to Peter." Now businesslike, she dug through her bag and handed me a list of séance participants. Sylvie. Peter and Tony, of course. Mrs. P. Bouncy production flunky Ashley. Dylan and Mikey, two of the tech guys. And me.

Sylvie and I sat at opposite ends of the glossy table for our chat, our reflections in the wood as upside down as our situation. I turned the list over. "I hadn't planned to be part of the festivities, Sylvie. Not quite my idea of a good time."

She fixed me with an opaque stare. "I thought you understood the agreement. Mrs. Parrish expects your full cooperation as a condition of employment. As does Mr. Proforta."

I made a graphic suggestion regarding Tony and his expectations. Instead of responding, Sylvie produced a file folder and proceeded to probe my responses to the questionnaire Tony had administered weeks ago. "I've already interviewed the others on the list, Ms. Livingston. For this to succeed, I have to understand the dynamics of everyone involved. I think I have sufficient insight into your personal dynamic, but..."

She wanted details to back up every answer I'd given. The tapping in the walls increased in volume until my head pounded, but Sylvie seemed unaffected by the noise level. Maybe the only one who heard it was I. At last, she relented. "Just as I thought," she announced. "You'll be trouble."

She must have been talking to Tony. "Then I'm glad to keep myself far away from your doomed Halloween shindig. In fact, I'm more than happy to take the day off. Maybe get my nails done."

"No, you can't do that." I felt her alarm laser across the mahogany. "Please. You're the catalyst, I'm sure of it. It's essential you be there to draw the spirits. We have to do everything we can to make sure they show up." She leaned forward. "It's live, remember."

I laughed hollowly at the irony. "I've kind of lost my spirit for the whole thing." Sylvie didn't laugh, but I really hadn't expected her to. "We have a full house now, as you must have noticed." The room grew perceptibly colder. "It would be a very bad idea to invite more."

Sylvie fixed her gaze on the room behind me. "I'm beginning to see your point.

CHAPTER TWENTY-SIX

Hallowe'en — or All Hallows Eve — marks the beginning of the darker half of the year. It is a time when the veil between worlds is thin, allowing easier passage from the Otherworld to this one.

In the uncertain light, I glanced around the dining room at the nervous guests, still wondering how I let myself be manipulated into this corner. Beside me, Sylvie Blakely, stark in black save for a rhinestone tiara and silver necklace, looked like a disembodied head. Peter, his golden hair a corona, sat next to her, the shadows emphasizing his flawless features, frozen with concentration. Mrs. Parrish, in contrast, rustled impatiently in her vintage silk Callot Soeurs gown. The sack style hid her frail frame, but the rounded neckline, weighed down by intricate beading, exposed the wattles of her thin neck. The bilious green color sucked any life from her complexion.

My employer had procured my dress, as well — a 1928 Madeleine Vionnet design of white silk satin. The sheath exposed a generous portion of my cleavage, which flounced unbound, since the gown draped low in back and tied below the hip. A square-cut crystal brooch gathered the bias-cut satin to one side, accentuating ample curves that would've been unfashionable in the Twenties. I'd been tripping over the train all night.

Across the table from me, Tony shrugged, uncomfortable in the white tie and tails he and the other men had donned to keep with the period. Flanked by tech guys, Ashley preened like a tropical bird, teasing them with her ostrich-feather fan. The strands of beads in her canary gown interlaced, delineating the perky young figure beneath despite the dropped waist of the design. Tony had been admiring the plumage all evening. He hadn't spared me a glance since the cocktail hour.

We were in the third hour of the ordeal, having filmed the segment with drinks and hors d'oeuvres earlier, recreating the ambience of the original night as closely as possible. As I limped about that first hour with a tumbler of whiskey, the strains of "I've Found a New Baby" floated through the sound system. Since I'd taken off my glasses to better reflect the era, I could only make out Tony's shape as he crossed the room towards me, oversized lapels shining.

"Shoe trouble again?" he smirked as he examined my sparkling antique evening pumps, which were tight in the toes. At least he hadn't called me Mrs. Livingston.

"I'm just a wardrobe malfunction waiting to happen. But I think that I can handle it." I'd always wanted to say something archly.

His smirk broadened to a genuine smile. "Gotta say, Mary Catherine, that's some dress you're almost wearing." He pulled the strap up, since it had started to slip. "Chilly?"

I took a long sip, welcoming the bite, trying to calm my reaction. "Not anymore. This is warming me up nicely." I lifted my chin and waited for the inevitable sarcastic remark.

Tony had been about to respond when Ashley flitted to his side, beads and breasts jiggling. I think her giggle chipped ice in the bucket nearby. Flirtatiously, she ran her fingers up and down his satin lapels, caressing his broad chest openly. "Tony, you are a burning beacon of raw sex in this tux."

Like that comment, the whiskey went down the wrong way, and I sputtered. Distantly, I felt Tony's wide hand pounding my bare back while I gagged into the snowy handkerchief he offered. So much for my efforts at brittle sophistication. I hoped that he'd edit out this part before it aired. As I staggered to the powder room, "Birth of the Blues" wailed from the speakers. Mercifully, I had no part to play the second hour, so I appropriated an ottoman to give my feet a rest while sexy Beacon Boy and Peter assembled clips and broadcast the background segment that led up to the actual séance, which was to be live at the stroke of eleven.

Apart from the choking, the evening had been uneventful—no orbs, no knocks, no bumps in the night. Sylvie and Peter fretted, and out in the van with the audio tech, D.J. was likely bored, but I was pleased as spiked punch at the dullness of the soirée. Even now, in the dining room, where the air was heavy with the scent of wax candles, nothing seemed out of the ordinary. Three night vision cameras peered from strategic locations about the room, capturing our every fidget and whisper. Following protocol, we joined hands. Sylvie's felt like dry sticks, but the meaty paw of the techie who squeezed my right hand was damp and sticky.

"Quiet. It is time." Down the hall, the clock struck eleven. Sylvie's breathing slowed. Her voice deepened. Around the room, the cameras' recording lights blinked red. My sense of relief vanished, and I gauged how many steps I was from the door, just in case.

"We desire communion with spirits of this house," Sylvie intoned. "We call you to the light, invite you to feel its warmth and enter our company. Commune with us." I cringed at the invitation. Why the hell was I here, a sitting duck? Why didn't I stay in the kitchen with Zina, calmly sipping tea and tuning out this supernatural psychobabble? I felt the techie shift in his seat beside me, dropping my hand before clasping it again beneath the table.

Sylvie was relentless. "Spirits of this house, come to us. Spirits of those who have passed on, join us on this plane." The tech's grip grew painful.

Then the candles flickered and the flames turned blue.

At first the tapping was insidious, an erratic beat, niggling around the edges of consciousness. Too soon, though, it grew insistent, louder, knocking until the table vibrated and I longed to reclaim my hands to cover my ears. The other participants sat in varying degrees of astonishment and fear. Peter looked stricken. The techies struggled to calm Ashley, who teetered on the brink of hysteria. Mrs. Parrish seemed full of wonder. Tony looked grim.

"Are you a spirit of this house? Tap twice for yes, once for no." I barely had time to roll my eyes at the cliché command before a fusillade of knocks followed. Dear God, how many were there? I checked my mental list of ghosts in residence, then thought back to the number buried on the next hill since before the time of the Revolution.

And Sylvie had just posted an open party on the spirit world's Facebook page.

Faint, then more substantial, figures paled in. By the gasps around the table, I knew others saw them too: a demented crone whose patchy scalp gleamed in the candlelight. A rigid autocrat in a black suit. A matron, face puffy and distorted, eyes bulging, hands to her neck. They hovered behind Sylvie, more coalescing behind them. I shut my eyes rather than see. My right hand throbbed from the bone-cracking pressure.

The shift came gradually. Instead of melting wax and sweat, the air now smelled of must and damp--an old smell, one I knew from years ago, one I'd sensed again in the cemetery the week before and remembered from that fateful bike ride. A smell of rotting leaves and wet stone and darkness. The stench of the tomb.

"Holy Mary, Mother of God," I whimpered, feeling the stink draw like a shroud around me, cold fingering my arms and banding my breasts. That same panic and helplessness I'd known as a girl came over me. This entity was not one of the Craggun family skeletons.

It was pure evil. It recognized me. And it wanted me.

I had to see. I forced my eyes open. On the table, the candles dimmed, as if a scrim had dropped between me and the light. "Pray for us sinners now and at the hour of our death." The darkness seemed a living thing, moving around me. I sensed its hunger.

The clock struck midnight. It had come.

The Day of the Dead.

CHAPTER TWENTY-SEVEN

Summoning a spirit back from the dead is a risky business.
Spirits, by their very super-nature, are out of touch with the living,
and the longer they've been incommunicado, the more harrowing
the reconnection can be.

"Remain in your seats. Do not break the circle." Sylvie could have saved her breath. No one dared to move, surrounded as we were by an ambush cutting us from the exit—if ghosts paid any attention to walls of plaster. The company's attention remained riveted on the specters circling the table—Grey Crag denizens, plus a motley mix in varying states of dress and decomposition, seeking the warmth of the living.

A soldier, red coat redder with his blood, partially dissolved into the figure of a young child, wispy hair framing delicate features—impossible to tell if boy or girl—gaunt and blue in a filmy nightdress. A haggard woman, wailing, belly swollen with pregnancy.

None of them seemed to sense the darker assault, a presence with them but not of them, that slowly cut off my air. Black spots formed and spread before my eyes. The blackness thickened, trying to gel into a shape. I thought I saw a pillar of black becoming an arm. An arm that was reaching for me.

"Holy Mary…" I prayed, frozen.

"Mother…"

The candle flamed red. Beside me, Sylvie jolted upright as if charged with electricity, reacting to this new presence. The bitter voice that spewed from her mouth belonged to one from beyond the grave.

"So this is what it takes to get you to call your mother?"

The blackness trapping me loosened its hold, drawing back, and I took a shuddering breath. No way. It couldn't be. "Mom?"

"Molly-Cat." The sigh brought back decades of pain as well as a flickering hope. Then I caught it — that long ago, dimly remembered scent of cigarette smoke and scotch and Arpège. It cloaked me, a tepid barrier between my pounding heart and the cold blackness that threatened. But it was a thin barrier, fluctuating, insubstantial. How could it hold?

"*My* baby." Now the voice came not from Sylvie, deep in a trance, but from the room itself, a croon, a declaration of war. My mother.

And war it was. The temperature plummeted and candles guttered, casting us all into a darkness so impenetrable the room itself vanished. Then the wind picked up, lifting tendrils of hair from my neck, blowing folds of satin, jangling beads. China clattered on the sideboard.

The blackness swirled, knifing about the room. Ashley's scream cut through the rumbles and cries. Cameras tipped, and tripods crashed to the floor. The dark was pressing, immense.

A flash. Across the table, a pinhole of light pierced the miasma. Tony had opened his cell phone.

Now dimly visible, a swarm of souls gathered. Parrish ancestors spanning generations flocked around their own. Mrs. Parrish's eyes gleamed, a triumphant smile transforming her face into a grinning skull. Around the room, other spirits clumped and whirled, agitated. The techie at my side keened. I could see his breath in the cold, wet air. Chaos reigned.

"More light!" I think it was Tony who shouted the order, and one by one, the technology came out—iPads, phones, Blackberry devices, driving the darkness to the corners. "Sylvie! Shut it down."

Tremors shook the medium, then convulsions, before a sliver of control resumed. "Spirits! You from beyond!" The swirling slowed and the tumult waned to a rumble. "Leave the living!" The rustling quieted. "Go. Go now. Go in peace. *Requiescat in pacem*." And, to my everlasting amazement, they listened. The gatecrashing phantoms faded, leaving behind only those ancestors surrounding my employer.

But against the far wall, the menacing darkness persisted.

Sylvie pulled at the chain around her neck, drawing forth a crucifix. She opened her mouth and I waited for another string of badly-pronounced Latin, but she had nothing. The dark thing didn't yield. In fact, it seemed to be growing thicker and darker as I watched. And it was advancing.

I couldn't sit there waiting another second. "Go away!" I shrieked. "Get the fuck away from me!"

With those words, the damp cold dissipated, the blackness lifted, and life flowed back until all that lingered were the scents of cigarettes and perfume.

A flood of light from the kitchen doorway finally broke the spell. Zina, fed up with the nonsense, was ready to clear the table.

CHAPTER TWENTY-EIGHT

"Why you mess with things you do not understand?" Zina turned in disgust from a shell-shocked Peter before putting her arm around me. In a corner of the kitchen, I hunched over an untouched cup of tea, warming myself in front of the blazing tapers on the altar. My mother's portrait gazed back unblinking. "Stupid men."

I had to agree with Zina, but at that moment, speaking was more than I could handle. Instead, I gently rocked myself back and forth, cradling my bruised right hand and watching the blotches bloom. I put my effort into forgetting that, at the beginning of the séance, when the knocking started, the tech guy had been holding onto Ashley. With both hands.

That, of course, begs the question: What had been holding my hand?

I did not want to think about this. Under the circumstances, I believe I can be forgiven for zoning out for a while. D.J sat close to me, strangely quiet. If I had been a better mother, I would have sent him up to bed, but I selfishly kept him nearby. In fact, I doubted I'd ever let him leave my side again.

There was evil in the night.

The world went on, of course. It always does. After a natural disaster, the National Guard arrives to restore order. In the wake of Grey Crag's supernatural disaster, Tony and his geek squad were still sorting out the equipment, recording the readings and playing back the broadcast. Poor Ashley, perky no longer, had been bundled into a taxi, gibbering. I idly wondered what the evening's festivities had done for the ratings, and whether they'd managed to bleep out the obscenities.

At least I could stop worrying about the potential law suit.

Mrs. Parrish had retired for the evening about an hour earlier, looking happier than I'd ever seen her. I refused to think of how she'd spend the rest of the night, since her entourage of dead relatives now trailed her wherever she went. Maybe they'd all climb into bed together. I gagged at the thought.

"There, now. It's all over." Zina's arm was firm. This was real. My son. The flame.

I watched it dance, the candle burning quickly, the flame stretching high, a thin plume of smoke rising above it. I had no idea how long I'd been watching the candle burn. I only knew it comforted me.

I should drink my tea, I thought. I should put D.J. to bed. I should light into Peter and Tony for putting us all at risk. I should. But I just stayed there rocking and watching the flame.

"How long has she been sitting here?" I recognized the voice, but it had lost its power to touch me.

"I don't know, Tony. A long time." D.J. sounded yards away, though I knew he was next to me.

"You okay to go up to bed by yourself? If I sit with her?"

"I guess."

I didn't feel Zina anymore. She must have left. I didn't feel anything at all, not even the cold. I hoped I'd never have to feel anything ever again. Imagine not having to worry or shut my eyes or cry or have my heart ripped in two. The flame could keep me safe and warm. But the candle had burned low. I wondered if, when the flame went out, part of me would be extinguished. Maybe it already was.

* * *

Slow circles on my bare back. Round and round and round and round. Warm. I didn't have to rock while the circles touched me. I felt wetness on my cheeks. Puzzling. My shoulders trembled. My eyes burned like the candle. My throat tightened. Beyond my control, gulping sobs shook me until I could no longer look into the light, but buried my face in my arms, surrounded by marigolds and skulls.

And still the circles turned, slow and steady and constant, while I cried for my mother and how I had loved her.

CHAPTER TWENTY-NINE

Effects of Paranormal Activity:
After facing an overly emotional spiritual event, some may experience stress as they try to make sense of the ordeal. Unless this stress is alleviated, emotional scarring may result. If care is not taken, new varieties of haunting may occur.

Warm and wet, the dishtowel gently wiped my face. When the tangles were lifted to bare my neck, the warmth was free to spread there, soothing. I felt drained, desiccated, the shell of an insect wrapped in a web. Timeless, I hung suspended between worlds without a twitch of life.

"Here, honey. Drink this." A cool glass against my cheek tricked me into opening my eyes. On the altar in front of me, the candles had burned out. The red wax seeped, hard and dry, onto the altar cloth, dots like drops of blood. A tentative dawn lit the stark lines of appliances and the drawn face and shadowed eyes beside me. Tony.

The tap water was clear, and I marveled at its sweetness after parched plains of grief. But with the water, the night flooded back—flashes of the teeming dead pressing in, sparks of terror, Ashley screaming, Peter surging to his full height,

Tony vaulting across the table and shouting my name. I shuddered and pushed the glass away.

"Drink it. You're dehydrated." Tony pressed the glass to my lips again. "More." Defeated, I swallowed, letting the coolness soothe my raw throat. "That's better," he murmured.

Well, I was glad he could be so damned optimistic. From my perspective, life sucked. And now that I was back among the living, I'd have to do something about it. "Is D.J. still sleeping?" I winced at the croak.

"He's upstairs. We texted for a while. He's worried about you."

"That makes two of us."

He pinned me with a look. "Three." The crease between his brows deepened. I studied him with surprise.

"Since when?" I was fully awake now. And riled. I hadn't detected any great dedication to my wellbeing on his front. Considering I'd been dangled as bait the night before, not to mention being used and left high and dry the last night we'd spent together, this current declaration rang as false as dipped pearls.

"For Christ's sake, Mary Catherine. We've been dating for weeks. Sleeping together. Of course I care about you."

I just didn't see that coming. "Dating?" I was at a loss. "We've been dating?"

He had the nerve to look offended. "All those lunches? Snacks in the kitchen? The hot sex?" He paced to the sink and back before adding, "Why do you think I hung around here day after day? We usually finish with a site in a couple of weeks." He was a portrait in exasperation.

Well love me tender and call me Elvis. "I thought I was just…a friend." Once I recovered from the initial shock, I was ready for round two. "When did you show up with flowers? When did we eat dinner in a nice restaurant? When did we ever even go out to a movie?" I threw up my arms. "I was a—a cohort. A sounding board. A consultant. An occasional release. And maybe a convenient accessory."

Tony bumped into the altar as I seethed, setting the skulls trembling and bottles clanking. "Mary Catherine, you are a lot of things, but convenient sure as hell is not one of them."

The morning light slatted into my eyes, prodding a migraine. This exchange was rapidly turning into the final act of a TV drama. And I'd had enough drama in the past twelve hours. "I can't do this right now," I sniveled, embarrassing myself. I must have looked as pitiful as I sounded.

Tony's face softened. "You should try to get some sleep. I'll call you later." He leaned over and gently pressed his lips to my temple. To my forehead. To my cheek. Transfixed, I closed my eyes, soaking in the sensation.

Kisses like rain.

Maybe dating wasn't such a bad idea.

CHAPTER THIRTY

The voiceover sounded tinny, and the images blurred in the low light cast by guttering candles. *Though details are sketchy, it seems our fellow tech star barely survived a séance that went horribly wrong. As you know, Mikey the Man is part of the tech support team for the now infamous Paranormal Posse. He took this footage when he was testing out his new Sony Ericsson W696 towards the end of the live broadcast Saturday night.*

I turned away from the monitor. I didn't need to see more to know that overnight, everything had changed. The images from the smartphone and TV broadcast were all over the Internet and now even on the local Monday morning show. Mrs. Parrish beamed, D.J. couldn't wait to get to school and share in the celebrity, and David was flying back into town. Sunday's conversation still rankled.

* * *

"How can you even consider staying in that place?" Even long distance, his voice packed a punch. "Even if it is all faked. It's...it's unhealthy. I want you out of there immediately."

"David, we can't just up and go. It's not that easy." I didn't have the energy to explain.

"Sure you can. It's not like anything's holding you there."

205

I wondered about that, remembering the brush of Tony's kiss at my temple, but David didn't need to know about my doubts. Squaring my shoulders, I tapped into my meager reserve voltage. "D.J.'s in his second quarter. He's doing better. He even joined the A.V. club." Over the last month, he had made a few friends, stayed longer after school, considered going to the football games. He was making a new life.

"So find a place to rent again."

Not in this pricey school district. I took a deep breath and proceeded carefully with a subject we'd never talked about. "What makes you think a new place would be any different?"

"That house invites nightmares, M.C. It can't be good for either of you. And it's in the same town where all the...incidents went on before."

I forced myself to continue. "By 'incidents,' you mean my mother's suicide? And the other...episodes when I was a kid?"

"Think of the publicity if the press gets a hold of that. What it could do to D.J." He knew just how to launch a threat so it hit a vital organ every time.

"Strange things can happen anywhere, David." The silence on the other end was telling. "David?"

"What are you trying to say?"

I took the plunge, even though I wasn't sure about what the bottom hid. "It won't matter where I go, you know. They're everywhere."

"The press'll back off in a day or so if you keep your head down." So willfully blind. He still believed he could control things.

"You know that's not what I meant." I lowered my voice. "Remember your Uncle Crawford's funeral?"

This time the silence lasted longer. When he answered, his voice was faint. "Yes."

"That wasn't the only time. It was just the only time I told you about." He took so long to reply, I thought he'd hung up. "David?"

* * *

Tony's arrival Sunday afternoon didn't help either. I trusted him even less than I trusted David. He looked me up and down, perhaps checking for signs that I might break into pieces. As if he had fared any better from the weekend's adventures. The bags hung purple below his eyes and thick bristle shadowed his cheeks and chin. Even his hair seemed flatter. The smile he attempted never managed to grow beyond a grimace.

Without enthusiasm, he sat at the kitchen table with his back to the wrecked altar and filled me in on Peter's latest PR plan. In the face of "irrefutable" evidence, the Paranormal Posse was expanding beyond the debunking business. Given the influx of new sponsors, the decision to occasionally track down actual ghosts made sound financial sense, he declared flatly, even if it held risks that should be obvious by now. He rocked back in his chair, waiting for my response, until I stood up and walked to the back door, holding it open. I didn't trust myself to say anything.

Tony, on the other hand, didn't seem to be able to shut up. "So I thought we might go on a *date* this week. For lunch. Or the museum downtown has a visiting exhibit. Two hundred Titanic artifacts." His eyes never left my face, which was just as well, since I looked awful in tattered jeans and D.J.'s NC State hoodie.

I shook my head in disgust and opened the door wider. "Titanic? Really, Tony?"

It took him a second to get it. I could sense the moment he understood when he grimaced. "I wasn't thinking. Sorry." He stood and took a step towards me.

I stayed where I was. "The death count was, what? Over a thousand?"

A step closer. "How about a walk in the park then?" The wind blew through the door, ruffling his hair.

"Valley Forge? Three thousand dead there." I shivered.

In the doorway, he shifted from side to side and stuffed his hands in his pockets, studying the flagstones. "Could be crowded, then." He cupped my cheek and smiled. "This dating thing isn't easy."

Fighting the impulse to lean into his caress, I stepped back over the doorsill and took a deep breath. "I can't date, Tony. Not now." Determined, I shut the door partway. "David's already calling me an unfit mother." I tried for a brisk tone. "And you've got what you needed from me. I was well and thoroughly handled." I glanced pointedly at my watch. "So thanks for stopping by, but I need to go." When I started to push the door shut, he pushed it open and stepped back through, slamming it behind him and reaching out.

His grip on my shoulders almost hurt. "You always say that. You're always running away. Not facing things." He turned my face to his as if he could will me into submission.

The fear and fury ripped through, fueled by disillusionment and a desperate need to retain some sanity. I tilted my chin and let fly. "Well, maybe things always work out in your world, Anthony Proforta. In your world of — of cables and lenses and EMF meters and ther — thermal scanners. You say you care about me. You have no idea what you'd be signing on for." I sickened at the memory of the dark entity that had shadowed me for decades and all the other horrors that prowled the edges of my vision. "And I can't—I can't do that to you. Us."

He still wouldn't let go or back away. "I can help, Mary Catherine. Let me."

I was sorely tempted, but I ploughed on, knowing I was right. "I can take care of myself. And D.J. The more I stand up for myself, the more alone I am, the more I support us and handle things on my own, the more I'll…I'll respect myself. And the safer we'll *all* be." I broke away. "Believe it or not, I have *some* principles." I choked down a sob. "Principles aren't just for easy times. They're for times like this, when we want something so much it—." I opened the door for the last time. "I can't date you, Tony," I said sadly. "You'd be dating the…the madwoman in the attic."

Damn him, he laughed. "I took senior English, you know. So now I'm Rochester?" He pulled me into his arms and planted a kiss on my forehead. "He got the girl in the end, right?"

He had. But he lost an eye and a hand in the process.

CHAPTER THIRTY-ONE

Understanding the Tarot – The Ten of Swords is the true death card, signifying a pain, a betrayal, and a final ordeal. It also represents, for some, an opportunity for martyrdom.

I didn't see much of my employer over the next several days, at least in person. I did see her on various screens, directing her carefully modulated Main Line drawl into the microphone, keeping her family history alive. She, along with Peter, joined the morning teams on all the local TV stations and granted countless interviews to reporters. Day by day, she looked less substantial, as if she were gradually fading into sepia tones. I worried.

Meanwhile, my job description evolved. I became her booking agent, fielding offers and scheduling guest appearances on talk shows. There must have been a lull in the Middle East and a dearth of celebrity scandals that week. Scars dug by mobile TV units capitalizing on the ratings rush marred the sloping lawn at Grey Crag.

Other scars were harder to see.

Unfortunately, I *had* seen David, who drove north and threatened to take D.J. back with him immediately. We crossed swords and parried. I reasoned. I argued. I offered

211

painful compromises. Although nothing I said made a difference, D.J.'s tantrums bought us more time—until the end of the semester.

"So you're jerking me around *again*?" D.J. stomped out of the back parlor into the kitchen, leaving David and me to trail behind. "Do you guys ever consider how I feel?" Where had the "you guys" come in? I was an innocent bystander in the current plan to ruin his so-called life.

David never found himself at a loss for words, another reason I divorced him. "It's for your own good, Deej." His tone set my teeth on edge.

D.J. turned to me, hands out. "Mom, can't you do something? You already dragged me away from my friends, and now that I've gotten used to it here, you're messing me up all over again." His powers of manipulation reached their maximum level.

My patience did too. "Way to pull the guilt trip card, kiddo." So I got to be the scapegoat this time around too, while David remained unscathed.

"All you ever do is order me around." His blue eyes blazed as he took aim. "You're bugging me all the time because you don't have a life of your own." That missile hit its target. I didn't have a life. And the future wasn't looking too rosy either. If David took D.J., I'd find myself all alone. Maybe Mrs. Parrish would let me adopt Penrod just to complete the stereotype.

"David, if you're really serious about this being in our son's best interest, at least let him finish out the term." I hated being forced to plead with David again. I thought I was done with all that. "He's been doing so well, and it's only another six weeks. How much difference can that make?"

Little did I know.

So we agreed on a tentative "wait and see" attitude, with a commitment to send D.J. south over the December break. That solution did little to placate our son. Had the house been less solid, the walls would have shuddered when D.J. slammed the door to his room, vowing to never come out. At that point, I'd seen enough of him anyway.

I had *not* seen Tony, who kept out of the way with David in the vicinity. I tried not to get my hopes up when lunchtime came and went each day. What did I expect? I'd told him we couldn't date, to back off, to give me space. How could I complain if he listened? And he was busy. With the whirlwind of publicity, Peter and Tony had landed their hot air balloon in the Emerald City, and they were rolling in green. I imagined that the extra money pouring in would keep Skippy deep in cheese wedges and let Tony hire a horde of decorators to refurbish his time-warped house—though he had no time for himself there. Or for me.

So like the weather, I was caught in a holding pattern between the richness of the harvest and the dead hand of winter. David went home. D.J. made a point of walking out of any room I entered and locking his door to shut me out, leaving me uneasy and exposed. Even the house felt restless. Though Zina dismantled her kitchen altar, the spirits roamed at will, no longer tethered to urn or banister. One awful morning I screamed when two heads peered back at me in the mirror as I brushed my teeth. Fortunately, once Mrs. P. was up and about the house, her entourage tended to follow her, generally leaving the hallways and stairwell clear. Only when she left the mansion, they occasionally sought my company, wanting something I could not give them.

I had nothing left to offer.

* * *

"Why don't I fix us a pot of tea, Mrs. Parrish? You've hardly taken a moment to relax all day." The tremor in her hand was more noticeable lately, and the blue veins stood out against her sallow skin. She looked both more fragile and more alive than I'd ever seen her, eyes glittering with an excitement that bordered on fever, despite the draft in the room.

"Oh, my dear, I can hardly take the time now. So much to do." The tremor increased.

Cautiously, I reached out a hand and drew her down on the sofa. "Surely you can take a break. How about chamomile and honey? Just the thing on a day like this." The last of the leaves had dropped, leaving maple limbs stark against the grey November sky. Even the geese had fled.

Relenting, she let her head rest against the cushion. "Well, perhaps a short break would rejuvenate me." Her papery eyelids fluttered closed and she sighed. "Yes, tea would be just the thing." She shifted, favoring her left side. "It might calm my stomach." She patted her sunken chest. "It feels like I swallowed a golf ball. Must have eaten too quickly."

A chill that had nothing to do with the weather slid under my sweater. *No, not this. Not now.* Mrs. P. absently rubbed her neck and shoulder. "I think I'll just rest here, if you wouldn't mind, Mrs. Livingston? About the tea?" A sheen of sweat coated her forehead. I knew these signs. I'd seen them in my father. Dread weighing my footsteps, I ran from the library.

* * *

"Mrs. P.? Here, swallow these." I held out the aspirin, all the while listening for the siren announcing the EMT service I'd called from upstairs. My own hand shaking, I held the glass as she leaned forward and drank. The effort left her limp. Holding her in my arms, I willed the ambulance to

214

hurry. She felt so cold, and up close her skin looked grey and mottled. From the window sill, Penrod twitched his tail and glared at me as if her plight were my fault. Perhaps it was. When we heard the sirens at a distance, Mrs. Parrish opened her eyes with effort, straining to focus. "You've been most helpful, Mrs. Livingston. I just knew you'd work out," she whispered and smiled wanly.

Behind us, her relatives stood vigil, somber and still.

The ride to the hospital, the phone calls, the flurried admission, and the labyrinth of white corridors all blurred together. I vaguely acknowledged the names of the doctors, the barrage of tests, the machines that beeped with each breath and heartbeat, the number of hours that passed. The one clear image is of Mrs. Parrish, pale and motionless, rehearsing for death in a sterile room.

For obvious reasons, I avoided hospitals when I could. Although they're dedicated to saving lives, they're full of dead people. I learned that the death rate from heart attacks in this one was about fifteen percent in a year, but the ghosts I chatted with said that's actually very good. The worst in the state is over 20 percent. What really ups the rate, they said, are the complications.

I came to understand complications through the rest of November. As days grew shorter, so did my patience. Even hooked up to tubes, Mrs. Parrish demanded I refine her family history, asking me to read new sections daily. At school, D.J. perversely chose to join activities he'd scorned for months, so I was obligated to ferry him back and forth. As the days dragged on, the posse came and went, and Mrs. Parrish brightened whenever they visited. On the days Zina came to the hospital with me, after she sat with Mrs. P., she and Peter wandered off to a nearby coffee shop. Everywhere I looked, people clumped in couples.

Tony hung back to talk after his visits, but our conversations were stilted, restricted to the show, the ratings, the holidays, even the weather. Anything more personal was off limits. During our conversations, he'd stand close, as if the force of his presence could somehow make me give him what he wanted, that just by being, he could wear me down. Resisting the comfort and safety he represented took all the determination I had.

I felt empty. Resolute. All month I declined his invitations to eat, pleading responsibilities. To Mrs. Parrish. To D.J. And to Tony too, who'd bumped into enough trouble on my account. Time dragged. Oh, the days were full enough. I even developed a routine. After I dropped D.J. off at school, I'd keep watch at the hospital and labor on the damned family memoir. In the afternoon, I took to dawdling in the kitchen with Zina until it was time to get D.J. But after dinner, when Zina had left and D.J. had retreated to his room, there wasn't a living soul around. That's when I weakened.

Twice I stopped myself from calling Tony. Once I even dialed David, who sounded distracted, probably by the woman's voice in the background. I tossed and turned in the sheets late into the night.

* * *

Tea doesn't taste right in a Styrofoam cup. I dunked the bag up and down, disheartened at the blunted flavor in the pale, tepid brew. The aftertaste was worse—acidic, coppery, tainted. I ordered it out of habit, feeling guilty at taking up a booth without buying something, needing to do anything other than sit and stare at the uniform beige walls of the hospital cafeteria. By the window, a scale model of the trolley line looked out of place. Like me.

Yet I'd been born upstairs, been treated in the emergency room, sat by my father in the surgical ward for the week he loitered before crossing over. My mother's autopsy had been in this morgue.

"Molly."

She cast no reflection in the Formica. This close, I could make out each eyelash. But she didn't reach out across the booth. I didn't blame her. We'd never been what you'd call close. And I'd brought on the thing that killed her — or at least drove her to kill herself.

My mother had always been careless, maybe even wild, dancing in the kitchen with her lush curls bouncing, hitching up her skirt to climb the school bleachers, chain smoking, telling off-color jokes at cocktail parties where she drank too much. She'd never been a Girl Scout leader. She refused to clean. She'd rarely baked cookies, and when she did, she ate most of the dough herself.

Now I knew why she lived life so fully. It kept death at bay.

In my mind's eye, I saw the pudgy kid I'd been, strawberry blonde hair in pigtails, tossing a pebble on a chalked hopscotch grid. The neighborhood playground teemed with children running, screaming, skipping, or scaling the monkey bars, while mothers settled on benches, laughing and gossiping and occasionally yelling or wiping a tiny nose.

One mother didn't sit with the others. She didn't even look like them with her tangled copper hair and tight shorts. While she smoked, she kept her eyes focused on her little girl, occasionally looking beyond her to the sliding board and then to the woods behind the playground. She waited, rigid and watchful, as the little girl tossed the pebble from block to block, teetering on one sneakered foot, bending, catching herself, and retrieving her pebble until she reached the eighth block and safely returned, the pebble still clutched in her small, sweaty fist.

I watched the mother spring from her seat and grab the girl's arm as she dropped the pebble. The child's mouth twisted in pain. "Time to go now, Molly-Cat."

"Bu-but we just got here, Mommy. The other kids don't have t'go yet. I wanna go down the slide." She looked up, still hopeful. "Catch me?"

The mother yanked the child's arm harder. "I said come on." She put her scarlet lips to the girl's ear. "It's not safe here."

The little girl's eyes filled with tears, but she stopped struggling and followed her mother to the car. It had begun.

That night, the news reported the discovery of a body in the woods beyond the swings. The shallow grave held a little boy who'd always loved that sliding board and now would never have to leave it, thanks to the pedophile who haunted the playground that awful spring. He was stopped before he snagged another playmate, thanks to an anonymous tipster.

My mother tried her best to stay out of the papers, but somehow her name leaked, and her role in the discovery made her a local pariah. I didn't get invited to many sleepovers after that. But given my newfound awareness of what hid along the edges of our lives, I didn't mind so much. Or so I told myself.

She'd kept me from the surprise at the bottom of the slide. She'd held me together that June evening when she drove to the cemetery and loaded me in the back of the station wagon along with my bike and—something else. She'd sat by my side in the emergency room, telling me to look away from the dim forms on the periphery, promising to keep them at bay.

After that, Mother didn't sleep. If I woke in the night, I'd find her in the living room wrapped in her gold satin robe, watching smoke drift from her cigarette, half-empty glass at her elbow. She drank with determination. And now I fully understood why. She saw, as I did, too much, alone in the dark.

Mother managed to hold the shadows back for six more months, keeping guard over the ones she loved in her own way. Until I left her.

"I'm so sorry, Mom. For everything."

Her eyes narrowed. "It's not over yet, kitten."

CHAPTER THIRTY-TWO

Funeral customs — <u>Stopping the clock at the death hour</u>. Originally, the custom came from Germany, and later, Great Britain, where people believed that time stood still for the deceased. If the clock continued, the spirit was invited to haunt endlessly, never moving on. Bells, the medieval forerunner of clocks, served the same purpose...

Mrs. Parrish lingered through Thanksgiving, time enough for complications to develop. She missed the annual oyster dinner for the Lower Merion Society for the Detection and Prosecution of Horse Thieves, but for 200 years it had continued, and with 500 revelers in attendance, the tradition carried on without her. Despite the busy social season, members of all the best clubs and leagues called by the hospital to pay their respects. Great nieces and distant cousins surfaced towards the end, and occasionally the old gal rallied enough to exchange memories.

She maintained her equilibrium even as her body wasted and the spark in her blue eyes faded and yellowed. She persevered at her death as she had through the tragedies of her life. By the time Advent arrived, even the air around her room was expectant. "Is there anything I can do for you, Mrs.

Parrish?" I asked, holding the brittle bones of her hand. "Anyone you'd like me to call? Anything I can get you?"

Her breathing had grown labored, so she merely shook her head and squeezed my hand. The grip alone remained strong. But one by one her systems gave up the ghost, and she too departed.

I hadn't been in the room to stop the clock.

She looked peaceful at the viewing, features smooth, like a linen tablecloth starched and ironed. She'd been laid out in lavender, a good color for her, flanked by lilies whose cloying scent thickened the air. I couldn't breathe in the confined viewing parlor.

Zina was a godsend those two days between the death and the funeral. Together, we faced our obligations, following Mrs. Parrish's wishes down to the last prayer card. Without my explaining, Zina understood the obstacles represented by hearses and mortuaries and maneuvered us through the hazards to pay our respects to the woman who'd provided a living for us both.

"So there's another chapel to your right. Just keep looking straight ahead." Zina kept her voice low, since a covey of Mrs. Parrish's social circle clustered around the register book.

"But there's one sitting right there on the left in that blue armchair," I hissed. "He winked at me."

She let out an irritated sigh and pulled me along. "Well, stay towards the middle, then."

"Do you see that toddler? In the corner? In the white dress with the teddy bear?"

She glanced up at me and pursed her lips. "No. Just keep walking. We're almost there."

But the little girl followed me with her eyes as I skirted past her. I lost it when she held out her arms, silently pleading to be picked up. Her mouth opened to wail.

Stumbling past the other mourners, I ran for the frigid air outside. The cold made no impression. I was always cold now.

Later that afternoon, Zina and I combined efforts to produce a post-funeral reception for the mourners, covering mirrors, clearing away tissues and fine white dust. In the library, I set out the volumes of photos, the scrapbooks, and the printed and bound manuscript Mrs. Parrish had so looked forward to. Now she had become the final chapter.

The funeral packed the small fieldstone church the next day. Mercifully, the casket remained closed, mounded with white roses. Around the coffin, arrangements clustered — gladioli, gerbera daisies, calla lilies, larkspur, carnations, orchids — sprays and wreaths and tall vases of tumbling blooms. Wet wool and melting wax and incense and roses choked the air, already heavy with dirges. My glasses fogged.

Once I caught Tony studying me from across the aisle. I looked away, remembering the last time we were together in this sanctuary. My cheeks grew hot. In the background, the service faded in and out. "God whose mercies cannot be numbered, receive thy servant..." My attention wandered to D.J.'s hair, which refused to stay tamed. One golden stalk had escaped the tines and gel, despite my repeated efforts. His blazer was short in the sleeves, exposing skinny wrists, and he tapped on his knee incessantly, as if typing on an invisible keyboard.

"Thou dost not willingly afflict or grieve the children of men."

The mix of sleet and rain led fewer to attend the burial on the hill. I sent D.J. to wait in the car and walked the gravel path alone, buttoning my raincoat and winding my scarf about my neck. My hair soon plastered to my head. Here and there, the occupants of graves stood by expectantly. I did my best to ignore them. Beneath the funeral canopy, Tony and Peter, overcoats whipping in the wind, bowed their heads.

"Look with pity." The minister's voice barely carried across the mound.

The artificial green grass seemed lurid in the grey mud. I knew a dark hole gaped beneath the unnatural carpet, just as I knew that worms and rot waited. Beyond the circle of folding chairs, more shadowy figures massed, waiting for the intrusion to end. I took off my wet glasses and slipped them into the pocket of my raincoat, choosing not to see.

"The earth and the sea shall give up their dead; and the corruptible bodies of those who sleep in him shall be changed."

I wondered how Mrs. Parrish would look the next time I saw her.

My feet had frozen in their black pumps, and the slick leather soles slipped back down the hill at the close of the service. To my right, the stand of mausoleums loomed, sleet pellets bouncing off their thick stone walls. I edged to the far side of the path. The day darkened. I wouldn't have thought I could feel any colder, but the air near those tombs turned blood to ice and stopped the heart.

Something moved, but no mourners lingered that bitter day. No sexton cleared dead leaves from the stones or scraped ice from the walks. No squirrels stirred in such weather. Not even the grave sentinels deserted their posts.

The black thing rose like a cloud from the hard earth dead ahead of me, obscuring my path. Behind me, gravediggers drew back the carpet to shovel dirt over Mrs. Parrish, trapping her beneath the ground. To my left, through a haze, I could still see the lighted church windows. The path was blocked.

So this is what death is, I thought. *A numbness beyond fear*. I wondered if this was how my mother felt at the end, drained by weeks spent waking and watching, like I felt after shielding my son and my frail friend from the entity that prodded and pressed to find a way in. I swayed, powerless to fight for myself. My last thought was that maybe the church could use the same decorations for my funeral.

"Jesus, woman, I can't leave you alone for a minute." A solid, living arm tugged at my waist. "You'll catch your death out here."

I started to laugh, a trill at first, then a chuckle, a gurgle, and something close to a sob. "You have no idea," I gasped. "Tony, hold on. Don't go any farther. It's back."

His face hardened and he scanned the mausoleums down the hill. "The thing from the séance?" I nodded, teeth chattering in the biting cold.

He pulled me closer. "Where?"

"In the path. Right in front of us."

His eyes widened as he looked ahead. "No shit?"

I wouldn't have blamed him if he'd turned and fled at that point. Hell, I would have.

"If I help you, can you run?"

I shook my head. "Not in these heels."

He glanced down. "Then take them off."

It was hopeless. He needed to see that and save himself. "Tony, it won't let me go."

Chin jutted forward, legs splayed, he assumed a gladiator stance. "We'll see about that. Come on, honey. We're going to make a break for it." The wind gusted.

Incredulous, I bent and slipped out of my shoes, no longer feeling the gravel and ice. Ahead, the entity swirled, condensing, drawing into itself, poised to spring. Tony pushed me behind him, putting his body between me and the thing that even now was shaping into something not quite human. While sleet pounded and wind wailed, Tony stood firm, looking up into the threat that only I could see.

He reached behind to grab my hand. "Ready?"

CHAPTER THIRTY-THREE

No. In no way was I ready for what came next—a rough scramble cross country, skimming plots and stones, skidding along the icy lids of crypts, snagging my scarf on branches, being yanked and pulled and carried while all around me, the blackness whirled. There was no path out of this nightmare.

"Come on, Mary Catherine. I'm not giving up without a fight."

But I'd already pushed myself beyond human limits. My pantyhose was ragged, my toes stinging, my legs wobbling, my breath uneven. "No more, Tony," I panted. "I can't. You have to let me go." I shoved hard. I couldn't let it get him too.

Then I wheeled to face the thing that chased me.

It stretched out an inky arm. I reeled and staggered, unable to breathe, my heart a fist in my chest. Behind me, Tony shouted, but I barely heard him. The thing lunged. I cowered as it sucked the life from the air around us, darker and darker, until all was void. The cold was all around me, pushing in. Regret flashed: D.J., forever fourteen. My failed marriage. Tony.

Then the church bell tolled. Its silver peal rang sharp in the winter air, clear and pure, cutting through sleet and darkness. The swirling slowed. I felt a tug of hope like a lifeline. Alive again, I stood my ground and grew a pair. It was high time I stood up for myself, so I might as well start now.

"That's enough!" I shouted in my sternest teacher voice. I was beyond angry. I was Fury herself, daughter of Night, and I had reached my last nerve. Summoning every ounce of ire at my command, I faced my darkness and my fears, determined at last to drive them back for good. "Get the hell out of my way! Abscond. Be gone, Cast off. Depart. Desist. Exit." I switched from English, just in case the thing dated back centuries. "*Fugite. Fyge.*" As I worked my vocabulary down the alphabet, the darkness dissipated, gradually lightening until I reached "Vamoose."

Then the path stood clear.

A bewildered Tony hugged me to him, and for long minutes we stood there among the graves, pelted by the blessed frozen rain, too cold to feel the victory. Then he led me out, supporting me past the tombs and through the gate to the car park where D.J. waited, ears plugged into his iPod. His head bobbed, and his hand beat time on his thigh. He didn't look up until Tony opened the car door.

"Took you long enough, Mom. I was about to come looking for you." I could've kicked him. But I didn't because my feet stung and because the thought of that darkness closing around my baby was worse than the nightmare I'd just lived.

"Give your mom a break, dude. It's been a hard day," Tony said. He settled me in the driver's seat, bending over to hold my frozen, bleeding feet. "You okay to drive?" I nodded my head, most of me still numb. "You sure? The kid could drive." I shook my head, not wanting to face possible death again so soon. He slid the shoes out of my petrified hands and shoved them on. "Got your glasses?" I nodded again, drawing them out of my pocket and wiping them on my soggy dress. "I'll follow you back."

Scant minutes later, Tony bustled us into the kitchen at Grey Crag, where Zina stood uncovering trays of food. Coffee and cinnamon and the stirrings of life greeted me. Zina did not. She just rolled her eyes heavenward, muttered about the grit and leaves we'd tracked in, and pointed to a chair. After depositing me in it, Tony turned and left. I didn't expect to see him again after what he'd gone through on my account. I slumped further in the seat.

Zina shook her head, hands on hips. "You look like a drowned cat." Hazily, I wondered what a drowned cat felt like. Maybe I'd ask Penrod when I found him. Probably upset by the flurry of activity after such a long period of quiet, he hadn't appeared since Mrs. P. died. Oblivious to the narrowly averted disaster, D.J. cruised the counter and piled a napkin with a sampler of funeral food before hightailing it for his room. Slowly, I peeled of my raincoat and followed him upstairs to bandage my mistreated toes, towel off, change, and ready myself for the next ordeal.

* * *

The weak December daylight that filtered through the drawn drapes in the library held no warmth, and even the wooden chairs groaned at the effort of bearing weight. David arrived, subdued for once, and he gathered up D.J., his backpack, and his computer and headed out before the weather worsened. I wouldn't see either of them until the week before Christmas—another loss. Midway through the open house, Peter stopped by, mumbling his regrets before seeking out Zina. I came across them later, standing close and murmuring near the pantry. I thought I caught Peter saying something like *muy bella*, but I must've been hearing things.

As guests filled plates with smoked salmon and scones, admired the displays, and wandered about the downstairs rooms, I hovered in the corners, alert and uneasy throughout the afternoon. Of course, there was no sign of Tony.

"The funeral arrangements were splendid, Mrs. Livingston. Just as she would have wanted." I rummaged around my brain for the name. Brassy hair. French manicure. Grey Givenchy sheath. Lainie. Lainie something. Some kind of cousin. She was the last guest, and I fervently hoped she'd leave soon so that I could collapse.

I managed a polite response. "It was the one thing I could do for her at the end, Ms. Barnhart. She was very good to me," I answered, throat sore. Maybe I was coming down with a cold. Great.

Lainie shoveled another canapé in. The tray was nearly empty. Surely she wouldn't stay much longer. She'd already inspected every painting and piece of silver. "So where will you go now?" She blotted her lipstick on the linen napkin as if she wished she could blot me up as well.

Now my chest hurt too. The question I'd refused to face couldn't be ignored. Excusing myself, I fled the library without answering her question, leaving her to pocket as many canapés as she could. I waited her out in the powder room, where I leaned my head against the door until I heard her car start. In the kitchen, I huddled next to the warm oven, hoping some of its heat would seep in. Zina's coat and bag were gone, so she must have left with Peter. Outside, sleet stabbed like daggers. I barely recognized my reflection in the dark pane, lank hair hanging to my shoulders, eyes wide and frozen, lips stiff, pale skin stretched across high cheekbones. Alone.

"Mary Catherine."

I saw him behind me, reflected in the window, sturdy and solid in a charcoal suit. "Tony. I didn't think you were coming back."

"Of course I was coming. I wouldn't leave you alone tonight." He held out a rustic bouquet of spiky purple blooms and pungent leaves. "Here. I brought you flowers." He smirked. "Since we're dating."

I smiled, knowing he was just being nice. "What a thoughtful gesture." I glanced curiously at the plant, stroking the fuzzy grey-green leaves. "I don't think I've ever seen flowers like this."

He stripped a leaf from the bundle, rubbing it between his finger and thumb to release its spicy aroma. "It's not really a flower. It's an herb. Sage." He waved it in a circle around me. "It's good for cleansing, Sylvie tells me. Keeps trouble at bay."

"Yeah, I'm nothing but trouble." I reached out to lay the herbs on the counter.

He laughed. "I like getting in trouble."

He could bring sex into any conversation. We had to be serious. "Tony, you can't keep trying to rescue me. You could be hurt."

He sure looked serious at that. "I'm already hurt." Before I could ask, he explained. "You told me to stay away."

I stood on shaky ground and started to slip. "I admit that wasn't easy. But it's not fair to you."

"I'm willing to risk it. We came out okay today, right?" A corner of his mouth turned up. "In for a penny."

"That's about all I'd be worth. This is no basis for a...a whatever it is we have. A hookup."

Tony moved behind me and wrapped his arms around my waist, looking over my shoulder at our reflection in the window. "You know you mean more than that to me." The tone was sweet, gentle, without the passion I'd once believed we shared but with tenderness I hadn't seen since the night of the séance.

My voice sounded flat in the echoing space. "Yeah, right." I'd learned from Jane Austen to beware how you give your heart. Determined and cautious, I stepped away. "Um, can I get you anything? There's still some coffee, I think." I started towards the cupboard, feeling rattled.

He reached up to brush my cheek. "Mary Catherine, stop."

The tears stung my eyes. "Stop what?"

"This." He tucked a stray lock of hair behind my ear.

It infuriated me. What right did he have to tell me how to feel or act or make me fall for him all over again? "Just what am I to you, Tony? Just something to handle when it's convenient?" I'm not sure if I fought Tony or myself. I just knew I couldn't take another second of this uncertainty. Hurts fester unless they see the open air. I'd festered for a month.

Tony balled his hands into fists. "What is this, some kind of test?" I could see his blood pressure rise as I watched. "Mary Catherine," he shouted, "you want to know what you are?" His face flamed red, and I steeled myself for it, for the final goodbye. "You're fucking unbelievable." Unable to refute the point, I waited for the rest.

"*And* impossible," he added for good measure. But then his shoulders slumped, and he raised his arms in defeat. "Impossible to live without. Do you know that when I got home that night after driving you here, I was reduced to scouting around for reminders of you? Your hair in my bathroom sink. Lipstick on a napkin. Wine on the bedspread. That red bra." He pulled me close. "You're funny. And smart. And cute. And this weird combination of dense and sexy that

I can't stay away from." He dropped his hands. "You're everything. You must see that. You're everything to me."

Maybe you've heard of stunned silence. I guess that's an oxymoron, but no other words could describe that moment. I wanted to run to Tony like the heroine at the end of the Gothic novel. I wanted to pour out how much his patience, his teasing, his persistence, his humor, his touch meant to me. How the day brightened when I heard him laughing. How I only felt safe when he was near. How I couldn't remember anyone else ever listening—really listening, as if I had something to say. How he'd filled all my empty places and how the idea of losing what we'd started had opened a black hole inside me.

I stopped, because admitting that, blindly trusting and hiding in those open arms would have been too easy. I needed so much more this time around. "Prove it."

Tony looked thunderstruck. "What?"

"You say I mean everything to you." I put the table between us. "But you lecture me on birth control, you ignore my new dress, you lead me on with cheesecake and sex and then leave me frustrated, you use me as bait like a minnow on a hook to reel in God knows what just so your ratings won't suffer, and it's been thirty-three days since you made love to me. That doesn't spell undying devotion."

"You want undying devotion? Since when?"

"Since always," I declared, crossing my arms. The silence stretched.

He lifted his eyebrows. "I was always better with my hands than my words."

I melted just a little, relaxing my stiff muscles. "That's a start, anyway."

His hands were warm as they slid up my back. His lips were warm too against my neck. I thawed a bit more, dropping my arms to my side. "Did I mention you're cute?" he rumbled.

"I think that came up." I closed my eyes and raised my face for a kiss.

He kissed each lid. "With eyes like pools of rain?"

The thaw began in earnest. "I don't think you mentioned that."

"I should have." His hands slid lower, and the flood waters rose. "And you have a really great ass." He squeezed gently and claimed my mouth, closing his arms around me and pressing me to him until I could feel every muscle hard against me. And I kissed back with all the repressed loneliness I had harbored, kissed until all I knew was his touch, his heat, and the heavy thud of his heart.

His arm was heavy across my shoulders as we walked up the staircase, leaning into each other, waving the sage at the body once again swaying from the banister. In my room, with the herbs draped from the curtain rods, he rubbed my cold, bare feet until I drowned with sensation. Only then did I shed the layers of black and wrap myself in him.

The bed still squeaked and the wallpaper still stared, but this time I tuned out the nether world and concentrated on the joys of this one. On the surprising softness of his hair and firmness of his shoulders. On the delight of kissing the folds of his neck and rubbing my breasts against his solid chest. On the intensity in his eyes as I ran my hand down his belly and lower still, hearing his breath catch and feeling him grow in my palm. I lost myself in him as my lips followed my hand and he shouted out before pulling me on top of him so we could ride out the waves together. The torrent surged, washing away the empty days and nights and opening the channel for something more.

And in the morning when we woke, the sun broke through, glancing off the icy branches, shattering the crystals, shimmering until the whole world held only light.

EPILOGUE

His first gift arrived twelve days before Christmas: proof in the form of a Tunbridge ware tea chest filled with the finest English teas. We sipped them from bone china as we nestled, calm and content, before the fireplace, watching the flames flicker.

I could get used to this dating stuff.

On the second day came shortbread from Scotland, a whole tin of my own. The cookies were cut into stars, and each one fit exactly on my tongue. I savored them and the sweetness they represented. Then rosy red Honeycrisp apples, which we ate in bed, licking the juice and relishing the tartness. The ensuing sex broke the bed frame. Wedges of cheesecake on Day Four followed the feast, and a bottle of Brunello di Montalcino for Day Five. But it was the new red lace bra in exactly my size that finally won me over.

I modeled it over a glass of the exquisite wine. There was never a more appreciative audience.

The house had been quiet as, well, a tomb. Shadows in corners remained only shadows.

Even my mother seemed to have taken off for the holiday season, which was just as well, considering how I was spending my nights. Zina still cleaned daily, waiting for word from the executor about the fate of her position. I passed the days putting Mrs. P.'s papers in order and packing, though I still had no plan for my next step.

The day before I was due to drive south, Tony made me an offer I couldn't refuse. We were back in the library reading the paper, poking the fire, and sipping eggnog. Bing Crosby's voice, like hot, buttered rum, sang "White Christmas" over the radio. Penrod curled on the hearth, tail twitching.

"Get away from there, you stupid cat," I scolded.

"Who're you talking to?" Tony sounded half asleep.

"Penrod. Mrs. Parrish's cat. That tail's going to catch fire if he doesn't move."

"Mary Catherine." His tone made me pause. "What cat?"

"You...don't see a cat?"

"No cat." He cleared his throat and leaned forward. "So...you see a cat?'

"There's a cat," I insisted. "A spoiled, fat tabby. Right there."

"Honey, I'm sure *you* see a cat."

"Oh." Penrod, ignoring the flames, sat up and licked his tail.

"Maybe now's a good time to bring up a proposal." My eyes widened. "A business proposal," he quickly added, looking flustered. "See, ever since the séance, Peter and I are kind of nervous about, you know, surprises. Sylvie's a help, but she's not what I'd call reliable. Detection-wise, I mean. Whereas you, you can detect a spook a mile away." I wasn't sure if I should feel flattered or insulted.

Nervously, he stood and fiddled with the fire screen. "So we were thinking that maybe, since you're, you know, between jobs, you might consider it. Joining the Paranormal Posse." He noted my expression and jumped in. "Behind the scenes, of course. Helping out with the preliminary investigations and such?"

And he named a figure that would keep D.J. in corn chips and high speed Internet and also pay for a roof over our heads in a decent school district. Looks like I had a sunny future in death.

In the morning, I packed what was left of my belongings into the trunk, knowing I'd never return to Grey Crag, but also knowing something better waited. As I cranked the ignition, I glanced in the rearview mirror. Mrs. Parrish, lovely in lavender, waved from beneath the dripping gargoyle, while Penrod twined between her bony ankles. I turned and waved back, not wanting to hurt their feelings. After all, I am the sensitive type.

ABOUT THE AUTHOR

Nancy Young strives to entertain, whether cohosting poetry readings, supplying interesting aliases at restaurants, or storytelling at Renaissance fairs. Although she grew up on the Philadelphia Main Line, she now lives in North Carolina, where she never runs out of material to jumpstart her novels, short stories, plays, and poems.

Her first publication was at age six, when her lion story was posted outside her first grade classroom. From then on, she was hooked, penning neighborhood dramas, improbable adventure tales, and Gothic romances through her youth. That love of the absurd and quirky never left her.

It also served her well for most of her professional life. Nancy taught literature, film, and writing at various colleges, earning awards for her instruction. She also worked as a journalist, newspaper editor, choir director, and mother. She married her high school sweetheart, with whom she shares three sons, a daughter, and a daughter-in-law. She counts them as her most devoted fans.

www.ingramcontent.com/pod-product-compliance
Lightning Source LLC
Chambersburg PA
CBHW020604180626
46810CB00007B/2639